Nick Jones is a retired journalist who lives in Herefordshire. After studying architecture he moved into journalism, working for Morgan-Grampian (formerly part of Express Newspapers) for 10 years, rising to become editor of the leading monthly magazine on restoration and refurbishment. He has published several short stories on the internet and work on his second novel is well under way.

KING'S CROSS

Nick Jones

Book Guild Publishing
Sussex, England

First published in Great Britain in 2015 by
The Book Guild Ltd
The Werks
45 Church Road
Hove, BN3 2BE

Typesetting in Perpetua

Printed and bound in Great Britain by
CPI Group (UK) Ltd, Croydon, CR0 4YY

A catalogue record for this book is available from
The British Library.

ISBN 978 1 910298 97 8

For Rae

Special thanks for assistance with the research for this book are owed to: the staff of London Fire Brigade; The London Transport Museum; Network Rail; Samaritans and Transport for London.

Contents

I

† *Arrival* †

UP THE DUSTY track, he slowly approached the gaunt white stone building. A faded sign, surmounted by a crucifix, affixed to the wall beside the huge medieval wooden gates announced: The Convent of the Little Sisters of the Divine Rosary. Crows squawked overhead and the sun blazed down.

Travelling from England by train, ferry and bus, it had taken Mark three full days (and some uncomfortable nights in station waiting rooms) to reach Siracusa on the east coast of Sicily. After two days exploring the old town, he had taken a bus to the isolated hill town of Solarino. Then he made the long climb to the sentinel-like convent, set alone on a rocky headland.

The tall, sun-tanned traveller stepped through the open gateway, pausing for a moment to enjoy the blissful shade. A nun clad entirely in white descended the steps of the main building and crossed the inner courtyard towards him. 'Mr Sutton? Welcome to our convent. We've been expecting you. I'm Sister Therese.'

The sister beckoned in the direction of the convent's main entrance. She could see that this newly arrived guest was exhausted from his journey, but she sensed that he carried a more ingrained tiredness. His clothes were casual – bordering on the unkempt – and his scuffed trainers showed the amount of exploration on the island he had done on foot. His dark, tousled, collar-length hair framed a rather forlorn face.

They crossed the square together and entered a spacious, stone-flagged hall, furnished with antiques. On the far wall was an icon that Mark recognised as being based upon Fra Angelico's famous *Annunciation*. It depicted the Madonna bowed before the Angel Gabriel, framed by two arches. Beneath the icon, in front of a willow pattern bowl containing dried lavender heads, was a small pile of picture postcards and a collecting bowl. Everywhere, the smell of incense hung in the air.

'Shortly, I'll show you to your bedroom upstairs, but first I should point out the entrance to our chapel there on the left; here is the refectory where you will take all your meals with us; and beyond are the cloisters, which we ask you to respect as private to the orders' nuns alone.'

'Of course, I understand.'

They climbed a narrow stone spiral staircase and arrived at a wide landing which had one side completely open to the elements in the Italian loggia style. Opening off it, Mark's room was just how he'd expected it to be: sparsely furnished, with a long leaded casement looking out across the hills. Beside it on the whitewashed wall hung an unadorned oak crucifix. He was relieved to note that the mattress on the four-poster bed was exceptionally comfortable. A water jug and bowl were on a bedside table.

His guide picked up a card from the table. 'Here, on one side, you will find the times of our eight services. Of course you are not obliged to attend any of them – indeed I imagine you won't want to rise at 3 a.m. for Lauds! On the other side are the times of the meals in the refectory, which we ask that you take in silence. Reverend Mother will welcome you this evening after Vespers. Now I shall leave you to rest and relax.'

'Thank you, Sister.'

After unpacking his small case, Mark stretched out on the bed and quickly dozed off.

He was awoken by the slow toll of the convent bell for Vespers and made his way down to the chapel. It was a simple service, conducted in Latin, with three psalms sung in the Gregorian style. Two rows of five white-clad nuns faced each other in the choir stalls, with the Mother Superior, in her purple wimple, officiating. At the conclusion, she led them out in single file.

Mark wandered up to look at the ornate, heavily-gilded altar. Behind it hung the convent's famous 400-year-old treasure: Caravaggio's altarpiece *The Madonna of the Rosary*, towering more than three metres above the altar's cross. He studied it for some time, marvelling at the intricate composition. Beneath a huge, pleated, horizontal crimson drape, a tableau of nine devotional figures, standing or kneeling, all faced towards a sublime Madonna – nursing the baby Jesus on her left arm – as she offered her rosary to St Dominic.

As he turned to leave, he noticed that one of the nuns had remained behind in the choir stalls, silently praying. As he passed her kneeling figure she looked up and smiled sweetly at him. Framed by her white wimple, her pure oval face had a childlike innocence. A faint smell of cinnamon and orange lingered in the air around the choir stalls.

The Mother Superior was waiting to greet Mark in the refectory doorway and guide him to a side table on which a cold buffet had been laid out. He was invited to serve himself first, before the other nuns took their food to their allotted seats around a giant oak table.

To the Mother Superior's right, an empty place had been laid, which Mark assumed was for the nun who had remained praying in the chapel. Following grace, the meal was eaten in silence. At the conclusion of the supper, two nuns remained behind to remove and wash the dishes, while the rest of the community retired to their cells for private prayer. Mark wearily climbed the spiral stairs to his bedroom and his first night in the convent.

II
The Goldfish Pool

MARK SPENT a fitful night, the many impressions collected on his arduous journey and the new retreat crowding his dreams. At one point he was awoken by what sounded like the rustling of a garment, but decided it was merely the window curtains blowing in the night breeze.

The following morning promised to be a classic Mediterranean summer's day: a vivid blue sky and the prospect of a high temperature. After breakfast, he decided he would walk the mile downhill into Solarino to buy provisions for his room and explore its back streets to find a café or bar.

Crossing the hallway on his way out, he noticed an archway which opened onto a small walled courtyard, in the centre of which was a pool stocked with goldfish. He descended a short flight of steps and sat on a stone bench to admire the fish. Occasionally they would break the pool's mirror-like surface to capture an insect or fly.

Though he had barely been in the convent for twenty-four hours, Mark somehow felt 'at home'; not through any strong spiritual connection, but more through the timeless tranquillity which seemed to suffuse his surroundings.

After some minutes of quiet contemplation he became aware of a figure standing behind him. He turned to find it was the young nun who had smiled at him in the chapel the previous evening. She looked serene, standing in the bright sunshine in her dazzling starched white habit. She looked down at him and smiled.

'Good morning. I trust you slept well last night?'

'Yes, thank you. It's so peaceful here, isn't it?'

'The convent or this pool?'

'Everywhere.'

'Indeed. But this is a special sanctuary of solitude for us.'

'Oh, I'm sorry, I shouldn't have intruded.'

'Please stay. You are our guest. May I join you for a few moments?'

'Of course. My name is Mark.'

She settled beside him on the bench. 'I know. And mine is Beatrice.'

For some minutes, they studied the pool and the languorous movement of the colourful fish in silence, until she spoke again. 'And you have come from England, I believe?'

'That's right.'

'What made you come all this way?'

Mark hesitated before answering. 'A broken heart. A lost love. Followed by some mental ill health which, I'm afraid, resulted in a nervous breakdown.'

'I'm so sorry. But you have come to the right place to recuperate. And you have chosen the best time of year for our warm weather. Though be sure to be careful of the sun during the middle of the day.'

'I will.'

Just then the chapel bell rang out and Sister Beatrice sprang up. 'I must go. I do hope we can talk again. Goodbye Mark.'

She was gone, leaving only a delicate scent of musky femininity and incense, mingled with cinnamon and oranges, hanging in the air.

After some minutes – during which he earnestly hoped she might return unexpectedly – Mark picked up his backpack and set off to walk down to the town. The gravel track's two distinct grooves indicated that it was wheeled carts rather than motorcars which used it the most. The temperature was already in the eighties.

Solarino was very old and had clearly once been a fortified town, judging by the sheer stone walls of many of the perimeter buildings.

All the roofs featured the distinctive patchwork of pantiles, set at jaunty angles, which are a trait of old Sicilian towns and villages. Many of the routes between the houses were mere pedestrian passageways; as they widened, the prospect of a sun-drenched piazza hove into view.

Mark found a small open-air market with stalls selling fruit, vegetables, olives, giant bundles of herbs and freshly-baked bread. He marvelled at the artistry of some of the displays: perfectly-sized polished aubergines, aligned like billiard balls and enclosed by sprays of fresh parsley and basil; criss-crossed ciabatta loaves, and plates of pitted olives, intertwined by bright orange chilli peppers.

In the centre of the square, an octagonal wooden *gelateria*, its louvred window shutters raised aloft, was doing a brisk trade in ice creams. He bought a double cornet of dark chocolate and strolled over to a shaded stone bench to watch the activity. The day was warming up and Mark realised it was going to be something of a race to consume all his ice cream before it melted and ran down his arm.

He washed his hands at the square's small fountain and then headed for a shadier side street where he hoped to find a quiet bar. Eventually he found one, marked solely by an ancient mosaic panel set into the wall beside its bead-curtain doorway, its tiny ceramic tiles realistically depicting a steaming cup of coffee. He took his compact camera from his bag and photographed the sign.

The café was empty and quiet. The back wall of the small space – there was seating for no more than ten – was completely taken up be an ancient copper and brass, six-pistoned Gaggia coffee machine, its top shelf neatly stacked with white china coffee cups. As if on cue in a theatre, the barista entered right: a tall, dark-haired twenty-something native Sicilian in a long blue striped apron worn over (it seemed to Mark) not much else, possibly panties and a vest. She gave him a welcoming half-smile, which was quickly followed by a dismissive, 'Oh, you're only a tourist,' look

'Una macchiato doppio, per favore.'

It was a good call. She swivelled around on her toes, setting her machine alight with switches and levers, noisily pulling down a cup and saucer and preparing to aerate a small aluminium jug of milk. The dexterity of this barista, Mark decided, was on a par with a church organist being unexpectedly requested to play a Handel anthem.

Hanging from a nail at the side of the Gaggia was a clutch of darkened tin stencils. She sorted through them, glancing back at Mark, as if to confirm her choice. Noisily the steamed milk was made ready, then delicately introduced across the hot espresso's surface. The selected template was then held above the cup, a sugar shaker of chocolate powder gently tapped across it. The completed confection was placed on a miniature tray and presented to Mark with a flourish. Alongside the cup was a saucer containing a single almond biscuit and a small glass of water. Etched in chocolate powder across the macchiato's surface was a crucifix.

'*Grazie*.'

After writing a postcard to his elderly grandmother in England, Mark returned to the square to find a postbox. There, in the heart of the market, he spotted the distinctive outline of Mother Superior, her purple wimple bent forward in earnest discussion with a stallholder. He approached with trepidation just as the nun was packing a large bundle of herbs, wrapped in newspaper, into her hessian shoulder bag.

'*Buongiorno!*'

'Mark! How good to see you. I am glad you have discovered our lovely market, and today is certainly the best day to experience it. Are you walking back to the convent?'

'Yes, Reverend Mother. May we walk there together?'

'But of course.'

As they slowly traversed the square, Mark appreciated the respect which local people clearly felt towards the convent and its principal. Most nodded or smiled as the two of them passed through the crowd. In England, to experience such veneration, Mark decided, you would probably need to walk through Manchester city centre arm-in-arm with Sir Matt Busby.

'So how are you settling in?'

'Fine, thank you.'

'And the meals in the refectory – are they to your liking?'

'Certainly.'

'That's good. I'm pleased. We live a very simple existence – some would say frugal – by modern-day standards and I sometimes worry that our guests come expecting luxury four-star hotel cuisine.'

'Well, this guest doesn't, I can assure you, Reverend Mother. And I think you do remarkably well, being so largely self-sufficient out here; you and just ten nuns to run everything.'

'Nine.'

'I'm sorry?'

'The order now has only nine nuns, plus myself. Once we were ten, but now we are nine.'

They slowly climbed the gravel track towards the convent's welcoming portals. Finally they reached the cool shaded archway and then the big stone-flagged hall.

Mother Superior reclaimed the shoulder bag which Mark had carried for her up the hill and whispered: 'I think we both deserve a siesta, don't you?'

III

The Night Visitor

THE EXTENDED siesta made up for his restless night. At Vespers, he decided to hang back in the shadows of the nave so that he might watch out for Sister Beatrice, although in the chapel's candle-lit gloom it was hard to discern her amongst the near-identical, chanting white-clad figures.

Once again, she failed to take her place beside Mother Superior at supper.

After the meal, he went straight to his room and read by candlelight for an hour or more, leaving his bedroom door half-open to create a cooling draft. Before getting into bed in his long cotton nightshirt he crossed the room to close it. Seated opposite on a leather chair on the landing was the figure of a nun, bowed in prayer, clasping her rosary. On hearing his movement she looked up and he immediately recognised Sister Beatrice. He nodded courteously, but not wishing to disturb her, retreated into his room leaving the door ajar.

He sat on the edge of the bed to reflect on the curious incident: why would a nun be praying outside his bedroom door when she had absented herself from the evening service? He was about to extinguish the candle when his reverie was disturbed by the creak of the door's hinge. He looked up to see Sister Beatrice framed in the doorway.

She entered the room hesitantly, then stopped at the corner of the bed, grasping a post with one hand as if for support. Confused, Mark remained seated on the edge of the bed.

'I shouldn't have come. I know it's wrong, but I wanted to see you.'

'I suppose I...'

'Yes?'

'I suppose I wanted to see you too.' He cautiously slid down the bed but didn't get up.

She took her hand from the post and placed it lightly on the nape of his neck, then stroked it tenderly. 'Mark.'

'Yes, Beatrice?'

'I just wanted to say your name. It's a lovely name; a very biblical name.'

'Come and sit beside me.'

'May I?'

'Of course.'

She moved to his side, dropping her hand onto his thigh, slowly sliding it up and down. She remained looking ahead. He could hear her breathing heavily. As he turned to look at her she turned too. Now they were barely inches apart. He felt her sweet-smelling breath.

Her hand stopped its movement. 'I think I should go.'

He gently placed his hand on top of hers. 'I think you should stay.'

'Do you want me to?'

'You know I do.'

She glanced coyly down at a growing bulge in his nightshirt. 'I can see you do!' They both laughed.

She stood up abruptly. 'Give me a few moments while I remove my wimple.' She stepped away from the bed and turned her back to him. She slipped off her crucifix, then dextrously unwound the starched white neck band and headcloth, laying them carefully on a chair. Then she tipped her head forward and shook it vigorously, causing a great cascade of chestnut-red curly hair to billow out. She turned to face him and smiled the same beatific smile which had first captivated him. He marvelled at her beauty.

'Better?'

'Amazing.'

After slipping her slim black shoes off she padded quietly towards him barefooted. She stood before him, took his head in her hands and kissed him affectionately on the lips. It was a long and tender kiss.

He reached out and unhooked her belt, allowing her white body garment to hang loose. With one shrug it slipped from her shoulders and then she was standing before him only in the lightest of shifts. He ran his hands over her buttocks, bringing her closer to his body. She pressed her breasts against his face so that he could feel the outline of her firm nipples through the fabric.

'Mark. My Mark. Be my lover?'

'I will, dearest Beatrice.'

She slowly slid his nightshirt up to reveal his erect penis. She raised her shift to her waist, then demurely gyrated to face away from him. Almost involuntarily, he spread his seated legs as she lowered herself onto him. Their lovemaking was silent but sensual, with Beatrice rising and falling in almost balletic elegance. Mark brought his hands up and placed them lightly on her shoulders in order to press her down on his cock as he came. She stopped her motion, allowing him to fill her.

She remained seated on his lap for some minutes, staring ahead silently. Then, snatching a serviette from the bedside table, she crumpled it into a ball, pressing it against her private place as she lifted off him. He marvelled at her lightness; she had a gamine figure and moved with ethereal grace.

'Lie on the bed, sweetest. I have an extra treat for you.'

He stretched out longways across the bed. With great agility she climbed over him, straddling his torso so that her beautiful rear was towards him. Slowly she lowered herself onto his face, perfectly gauging it so that her labia lips engulfed his mouth, like the petals on an exotic plant.

At the last moment she withdrew the napkin, releasing Mark's newly-planted seed, allowing him to experience an erotic 'cream pie'. She slowly ground her buttocks onto his face, rocking her clitoris against the bridge of his nose, then quivered as her orgasm arrived. It was animalistic, but hugely sensuous.

Several minutes passed as they remained locked together in silent awe. Finally, she rose off him, alighted to the floor, then leant forward to kiss him tenderly.

'My own Mark,' she whispered. 'My lover. I will always watch over you.'

He closed his eyes, bewitched and exhausted, and quickly lost consciousness.

He was awoken by the chapel bell tolling for Lauds, but Beatrice was gone, along with her habit and wimple and shoes. Only the crumpled napkin lying on the stone floor – and the tantalising smell of her scent – were evidence of their love-making.

IV

Revelation

BREAKFAST in the convent refectory was a straggled affair, with the nuns eating only bread and drinking watery coffee from a communal jug, before leaving to undertake their morning domestic or gardening duties. Beatrice did not appear and Mark decided to go for a long walk up the hill behind the convent.

He struck out along a hot, rock-strewn path, his shirt now tied around his waist, heading for a cool-looking olive grove at the crest of the hill. He passed three nuns toiling in a field, dressed in hessian habits and cowls and wielding ancient harrows. Their stooped manner and bulky shapes convinced him that none were his Beatrice.

On reaching the ancient olive grove, with its crooked tree trunks already straining under the weight of the ripening fruit, Mark sought a shady corner beside a dry stone boundary wall. Tiny lizards happily chased each other in and out of the cracks between the stones, while house martins swooped and dived overhead.

He pulled a bag of mixed nuts and raisins from his pack and took a swig of water. The experience of the previous night and the upsetting disappearance of Beatrice troubled him. He pondered over her whereabouts and why she had deserted him so abruptly when she could have remained by his side until the morning.

On his return to the convent he glanced at the walled goldfish pool enclosure, hoping that his lover might be sitting demurely praying, or in meditation, but the stone bench was empty. Neither did she attend the Sext service which always preceded lunch.

He went to his room without eating. For Vespers, Mark took his place at the end of the choir stalls and though the light was now fading he was certain Beatrice was still absent. A whole day without seeing her. He began to fret that she was unwell.

Supper was taken in silence. Once again, the place laid at the table beside the Mother Superior remained unoccupied.

As the nuns rose to return to their cells to pray privately, Mark hung back, hoping to speak to the Mother Superior. They left the refectory together and she paused in the hallway.

'And how are you finding your stay with us, my child?'

'Very restful, thank you, Reverend Mother. Very therapeutic.'

'Good.'

'Errr...may I ask a question?'

'Of course.'

'At your side at the refectory table there is always an unoccupied place, set out with cutlery, bowl and glass. Whose place is that?'

'Sister Beatrice's.'

'And why does she not join us for meals?'

'Because she is dead.'

Mark froze with a chilling shudder. 'Dead? Sister Beatrice dead?'

'Yes, my child. Poor Beatrice left this earth exactly two years ago last night. Her place at table is our memorial to her memory.'

'But how did she die?'

She crossed herself before answering. 'By her own hand.'

'How?'

'The poor child – who had been disturbed ever since her parents from the little town below brought her to us when she was thirteen – discovered some sleeping tablets left by a thoughtless guest in one of the bedrooms. She took the whole bottleful. We found her seated where she had taken them.'

'And where was that?'

'In the leather chair on the landing, opposite your bedroom.' Mark remembered Beatrice's final words.

V

The Long Walk

MARK's restless night was filled by fitful bursts of distorted images of Beatrice. Each time he managed to wake himself from these dreams, he looked towards the door of his bedroom, hoping to see her svelte figure framed in its opening.

He rose just before dawn and after washing and dressing, went down to the convent chapel just as Matins was ending. He stepped back into the shadow of an arch as nine nuns filed silently past. After collecting some bread and fruit from the refectory, he dejectedly returned to his room.

For three more days he kept himself to himself, dividing his time between long sessions of meditation alone in the chapel, or reading in his room. Supper was the only meal he took with the nuns in their refectory.

He was now resigned to the fact that there was little likelihood of Beatrice reappearing. In an effort to break his morbid reverie, he decided he would take a long, all-day hike up into the hills behind the convent. Armed only with a backpack and stick, he set off shortly after 9 a.m. It was already warm and the portents – high streaky cumuli – were for a very hot day.

He made good time to the olive grove, then struck out on a new and untried track running alongside a deep, shaded ravine, at the bottom of which was a stream. It looked so inviting down there, but the thought of the subsequent ascent deterred him and he walked on. With the sun climbing higher, the shadows of trees and shrubs – and their welcoming shade – became sparser.

He stood with his back pressed against the coolness of a high rock escarpment to eat an apple. A tiny lizard scurried away in fright. Nearby, lying on its side in some brambles, was the rotted wooden chassis of an iron-wheeled trolley. Some sort of industrial barrow, Mark conjectured, though what possible industrial use it had performed in this godforsaken landscape, he couldn't fathom. He noted that its rusted iron wheels were flanged rather than flat, indicating that it had once run on rails.

Beyond his right shoulder, there was a large opening in the rock face, its entrance worn smooth by wind erosion. He moved down to investigate. It seemed to be a natural cave. He stood first in its entrance, then cautiously went inside.

His feet crunched on old dry leaves which the wind had blown in. He paused to allow his eyes to adjust to the sheer blackness within. Without a torch or lighter, he was reluctant to venture more than a couple of faltering steps forward. He raised a hand to check that there were no overhanging rocks to hit his head on. The cool interior of the still blackness was certainly welcome, but the cave's acrid mustiness was unpleasant. It reminded him of the smell of a dog which jumps into a stagnant pool and immediately jumps back out, shaking its coat violently.

Then he heard a noise. A soft, tentative shuffling had disturbed the dried leaves further inside the cave and a slowly approaching movement told him he was not alone. He held his breath. Could it be a rat? Even a snake? The movement stopped. He and the other 'occupant' of the cave had sensed each other's presence; both now remained motionless.

Deciding that fresh air – even at thirty degrees – was preferable to the smell of damp dog and mysterious footfalls, he stepped back into the dazzling sunlight.

With the sun now approaching its zenith he pressed on, but soon regretted the decision when the track petered out into a barren, rock-strewn plateau. The flat, treeless vista ahead positively shimmered. He knotted his handkerchief into an ineffective sun hat and after stumbling for a third time on loose rocks, decided to re-trace his steps and call it a day.

The descent was certainly easier, though he was now starting to feel light-headed. He took the last apple from his backpack but his water flask was empty. There were no trees or shady rocks for refuge from the sun's pounding heat and the twinkling Ionian Sea in the distance beyond Syracusa looked so inviting.

But for the gradual downward gradient, he would not have known in which direction to walk. He had scuffed one of his knees and it was now weeping blood, forcing him to remove his 'sun hat' in order to bandage it.

The azure blue sky began to darken very rapidly. It was as if Zeus had decided to pull a celestial roller blind across the heavens to create a gloomy atmosphere. Far to the north, where Etna dominated all of Sicily, vivid horizontal forked lightening zig-zagged across the darkening sky. Then came a crashing boom of thunder. The storm's southward approach was unexpectedly rapid, like a train on the London underground emerging from a tunnel, and just as noisy.

In less than two minutes, Mark was desperately searching for a refuge from the vertical deluge. The track he was walking on, which had previously been a benign sandy trough, was now a fast-flowing rivulet of orange storm water. He casually noted that the laces of his half-submerged trainers were the same colour.

Through the sheeting rain he could just make out the familiar outline of the olive grove's ancient trees. If he pressed on through the downpour, he calculated that he had no more than ten minutes to reach its entrance gates. From there it was a short distance back to the convent.

He finally made it to the grove, collapsing on the ground beside the shelter of a boundary wall. The rain began to ease and as the blue skies returned, he dozed off. When he awoke – he couldn't tell whether he'd been unconscious for a few minutes or an hour – he had a raging headache and felt giddy. With his back pressed against the wall, he took several deep breaths in an effort to gain the strength to stand up and stagger back to the convent. At the third attempt, he was up.

As he clutched one of the coping stones on top of the wall for support, his eye was caught by a flickering red movement in an olive tree in the bottom corner of the grove. Since he had to walk in that direction, he stumbled forward to investigate.

The 'red alert' turned out to be a long ribbon flapping in the breeze, attached to the hat band of a straw hat which was hanging from a low branch on one of the olive trees. He lifted it down and was surprised to discover that, despite the thunderstorm, it was bone dry and in near-pristine condition. And it fitted him perfectly. Its unexpected acquisition gave him the renewed energy he needed to press on and regain the protective sanctuary of the convent.

As he approached the opened wooden entrance gates of The Convent of the Little Sisters of the Divine Rosary, the bell for Vespers began ringing. He stepped into the shade of the gateway at the very moment that his legs turned to rubber and he keeled forward unconscious into the dirt.

VI

Fever

HE AWOKE in his bed just before dawn, having slept for over eight hours. His head ached and beneath the bed sheets a neatly-bandaged knee was nagging and painful. With vague recollections of passing out in the convent's gateway, he puzzled over how he had managed to climb the narrow spiral staircase, undress and get into his nightshirt – and bandage his own knee.

The answer to these conundrums was very soon provided by the arrival of Sister Lucia, carrying a breakfast tray containing a mug of coffee, a warmed and buttered ciabatta roll and an orange. 'We had quite a job getting you up the stairs, Mark, I can tell you.'

'However did you manage it?'

'It was Reverend Mother's idea. We got you seated on one of the refectory chairs while you were still out cold, then four of us took a chair leg each and brought you up here.'

'And err...who put me to bed?"

The sister leaned across and pumped up his pillows. 'We left that to Reverend Mother.'

'Well, thank you, all of you. Really, I don't know how I managed to get myself into such a state.' He glanced across at his dust-covered trainers in the corner.

'Reverend Mother says it's a simple case of sunstroke and that you're going to have to stay put in bed for at least two days. Good job you had your hat, that's all I can say.'

'Hat?' At the same moment that he asked the question he saw the straw boater, hanging jauntily from a hook on one of the bed posts, its red ribbon dangling below.

Sister Lucia glanced in the same direction. 'Did you get it in Venice?'

'Venice?'

'Why yes. That's a proper gondolier's hat. They only make them in Venice.'

'No. I found it in a tree.'

'In a tree? Whereabouts?'

'Up in the old olive grove above the convent. It was hanging on a branch of one of the trees. Maybe it belongs to the man who owns the grove?'

'I very much doubt it, my dear. Old Signor Mansini lives on the mainland. Only comes over here at harvest time. Any case, he's such a stingy old buzzard he'd never leave an expensive hat like that in one of his trees. How far did you walk altogether?'

'Oh, way beyond the olive grove. Along the side of a deep ravine and then I climbed up a track until I reached a plateau.'

'Scrubby with gorse and rocks?'

'Yes. That's when I fell and cut my knee.'

The old nun crossed herself. 'Well it's a miracle you ever returned!'

'What makes you say that? Are there snakes in the gorse?'

'Wild dogs!'

'Dogs?'

'Horrible great beasts the size of small ponies, with sleek black coats and big ugly muzzles. Some say they've been up there since Roman times. Live totally in the wild and hunt in packs like wolves. With your knee bleeding they'd have been onto you in an instant. Torn you apart, limb from limb, they would.'

Mark was beginning to wonder if his nursing visitor was a bit of a fantasist. 'Has anyone ever seen these animals?'

'Some of the nuns say that in the years when we've had hard winters, two or three of them will come down and lurk around near the convent, in the hope of picking up food scraps. But I've not seen them.'

'And where do these dogs live?'

'Up below the plateau you were describing. There are several openings in the rocks; they look like caves but they're actually disused copper mine workings. They're said to live in one of those.'

Mark finished his coffee. The mystery of the gondolier's hat – which had probably saved his life – remained unresolved and Sister Lucia shuffled off with the empty breakfast tray, muttering to herself about the dogs. Mark rested his head on the pillows and soon dozed off.

When he next opened his eyes, he saw the familiar, purple-clad figure of the convent's Mother Superior seated at his bedside in prayer, clasping her rosary.

She looked up and smiled at him. 'You've been asleep all day.'

'What time is it?'

'Shortly before Vespers.'

'But it only seems like five minutes ago that Sister Lucia left with my breakfast tray.'

'Nine hours ago, my child. Still, it's a good sign. Your body is recovering. But I think you need to stay here in your room for one more day.'

'Shall I come down to Vespers?'

'No, tomorrow. I will bring you your supper after the service. And if you are up to it, Mark, I think we should have a little talk.'

'Certainly, Reverend Mother.' Although he agreed to the suggestion, he was at a loss to know what the subject of their talk would be.

She stood up and straightened her habit. 'Now I shall leave you for an hour.'

Mark closed his eyes and was soon asleep again. He was gently awoken by the sweet aroma of a bowl of beef and lentil broth, sitting in the centre of a tray which had been placed on his bedside table. He dipped the end of a ciabatta roll into the soup and eagerly began consuming it. This time, the Mother Superior stood back from the bed, eyeing him in a matronly manner.

'How are you feeling?'

'Much better, Reverend Mother, thank you. Definitely on the mend, I'd say.'

'You had a lucky escape, Mark. Some would say miraculous.'

He mopped up the last of the broth with bread. 'I know. And I can't tell you how much I appreciate all you and Sister Lucia and the others did for me. I shall always be in your debt.'

She approached the bedside, removed the tray and sat down. She stroked her habit free of creases then coughed nervously. 'With another day's rest, I think it will be all right for you to join us in the refectory for your meals. And perhaps attend one of the services?'

'Of course.'

'Mark, this is a very insular place, my child. The phrase "closed order" indicates that, so we may be closer to God, we have cut ourselves off from the outside world, to all intents and purposes. But, as I expect you know, all orders such as ours are bound by the Rules of St Benedict, and we will never refuse shelter or succour to a traveller. Therefore, feel free to remain here as long as you want.

'My main concern is that our cloistered way of life could add to your introspection; remaining here for too long might hamper your psychological recovery. You are still young, with your life ahead of you – unlike most of us! So when you feel you are ready to move on, just come and see me and I will make the necessary travel arrangements.'

They sat together in silence. After a long interval she asked: 'Tell me, will you have a job to go to when you eventually return to England?'

'Nope. My last job ended abruptly earlier this year. I managed an art gallery in a posh London district called Belsize Park. I have an arts degree.'

'Indeed? And which period of art history did you study?'

'Sixteenth and seventeenth century Italian schools, but in particular the work of the great Michelangelo da Caravaggio.'

The Mother Superior smiled. 'Ah, so it was no coincidence then that you wrote to me asking if you could come on retreat to our convent?'

'No. I knew the history of your altarpiece, of course. And also of the one in Siracusa, *The Burial of Santa Lucia*, which I went to see before coming up here.'

The Mother Superior looked down on him with compassion. After a minute's reflection she said: 'You and the great artist, it seems to me, have two common particularities.'

'Oh really? And what are they?'

'You're both headstrong and accident-prone! And of course in Caravaggio's case, as we both know, that proved to be a fatal combination.' Mark had no answer.

'So, tell me, what happened to this art gallery that you were running in London?'

'It folded – closed down, due solely to the proprietors' greed. I was given one's week's notice, and no financial compensation.'

'But you had somewhere to live?'

'Well, that was really the start of my problems and why I started to crack up. Maggie, my partner of six years, announced that she wanted to split up as she'd fallen in love with someone else. This was in the same week that the gallery owner told me he was closing. They say problems often come in threes, so I suppose my nervous breakdown was the third!'

'Well, you are to remember, Mark, that you may stay with us for as long as you want.'

The light in the room was now fading and Mark stared fixedly ahead. Looking over the Mother Superior's shoulder towards the half-opened door, he could just make out the form of the leather chair on the landing. The chair in which Beatrice had been sitting praying on the night they had made love together. The chair where she had taken her own life.

'I'm sorry. I was miles away. What did you say?'

'I said that you may stay with us for as long as you want.'

He continued to stare at the chair. 'Err...yes, that's very kind of you, Reverend Mother, I...'

He broke off as he felt his body temperature fall rapidly, with a tingling sensation around his shoulders and neck. Sister Beatrice was now seated in the chair, looking adoringly into the bedroom towards him and smiling. He put a hand to his mouth as if to stifle any cry of the recognition of his lover.

'I sense that you're tired now, Mark. I should not have talked to you for so long. I'll take the tray and leave you to rest.' The Mother Superior rose and removed his tray.

As the chapel bell for Compline began to toll, the vision on the landing vanished.

Once again, Mark's night was fitful and plagued by strange demonic dreams. The more gruesome images of the Caravaggio paintings he knew so well became melded into scenes in and around the convent. Twice he awoke with a start, sure that someone was moving stealthily around the four-poster bed.

Once he called out. But both times he reasoned that it was only the long curtains flapping in the cooling night air. He heard the bell for Matins, but his limbs refused to obey his command to get up and go down to the chapel. Then it was dawn.

For Mark's second day of confinement, Mother Superior assigned Sister Concetta to take him his breakfast tray. She had set it on the bedside table as he was still asleep. When the nun returned half-an-hour later, Mark had consumed all the food.

'Reverend Mother asks if you are feeling any better today?'

'Yes, thank you, Sister. Tell her I would definitely like to attend Vespers this evening and join you in the refectory afterwards.' He handed her the tray.

'Before you go, can I ask you, Sister...'

'Concetta.'

'Sister Concetta. Did you by any chance know Sister Beatrice?'

'Yes, I knew her well. In fact we grew up in Solarino together – we were the same age and went to school together. You could say we were almost like sisters.'

He studied the little nun's similar oval-shaped face, framed by the white wimple. He even imagined that it could have been the two of them he'd first seen, seated together in the chapel's choir stalls.

She looked down at her shoes nervously. 'It was such a desperately sad business. I still miss her terribly.'

Mark sensed it would be tactless to pursue the conversation any further and was about to change the subject when Sister Concetta brightened up.

'Although I say we were like sisters – in physique and temperament, and in our spiritual feelings and beliefs – there was one thing that marked us apart.'

'And that was?'

'Beatrice's hair. Beneath her wimple was this amazing cascade of the most lustrous chestnut-red curls, which of course were only visible when she undressed to go to bed.'

Without checking his response Mark said: 'I know.'

Concetta looked at the window, initially in disbelief at the Englishman's remark, then dismissing it as a slip of the tongue. She quickly found an excuse to leave the room with the tray and return to her kitchen duties.

Mark decided to use the morning to explore some of the rooms which opened off the convent's square-shaped, open-sided landing, which overlooked the central courtyard. He washed and dressed and recovered his sketching book and pencils from his suitcase. As he stepped out onto the landing, the distant clink of crockery from the kitchen told him that the nuns were busy with washing-up and the preparation of the day's meals. Pigeons cooing on the pantiles added to the air of tranquillity.

There were single bedrooms beyond his, their doors ajar and beds unmade. Then a larger and more ornate room – perhaps reserved for visiting church dignitaries – which had a baroque plastered ceiling. Above the carved mahogany bedhead was a wonderful crucifix, its edges encrusted with jade and mother-of-pearl.

He studied the ceiling more closely. Myriad cherubs ringed its edge, with the centrepiece a garlanded Madonna, her arms spread open in supplication. The craftsman who had created this work had clearly been influenced by the convent's altarpiece, though here the infant Jesus was absent. He found a chair and sat sketching the ceiling's pink-washed plaster reliefs for more than an hour.

Hearing approaching footfalls, he put down his pad and pencil and went out onto the landing, expecting to find either Sister Concetta or the Mother Superior. There was no-one to be seen, and the flapping of two mating pigeons' wings made him dismiss the notion that there was anyone around.

After collecting his sketching things he continued his tour, returning to his room shortly before Sister Concetta appeared (now fully composed after her earlier discomfort) with a lunch tray. In an effort to restore an air of equanimity, Mark asked: 'Do you suppose Reverend Mother would mind if I sat by the goldfish pool after lunch? I do so like that space.'

'I'm sure that would be all right. But do remember to take your hat.'

In the quiet hour before the None service – an hour when many of the order's older members took a nap in their cells – Mark descended the stone staircase to the entrance hall and out into the walled enclosure of the fish pool. Its white sandstone walls radiated bright light and warmth. His straw hat was certainly essential.

He took his place to one side of the two-seated bench which looked towards the pool, though even the goldfish seemed to be having a siesta. He glanced down to his left, almost expecting the other half of the seat to be occupied by his spectral lover. Doves fluttered languidly in the branches of a nearby cypress tree. With no distractions from the sisters and even Nature itself half-asleep all around him, this seemed the perfect time to consider his future. To stay or move on.

Apart from the brief initial 'sighting' in the chapel on the evening of his arrival, Mark and Beatrice had 'met' twice – once by this pool and once when they had made love together in the night. This troubled young woman had spent her entire adult life within the walls of the convent and had chosen to end it here. If he followed the Mother Superior's advice and returned to England, he would surely be turning his back on Beatrice. There was really not the remotest expectation that he would ever see her again. And yet.

And yet. To moon about like some love-struck Romeo, in the hope of catching a fleeting glimpse of a shadowy figure, or to hear the scamper of her tiny slippered feet on the bedroom's stone floor in the middle of the night, was patently absurd. Suddenly, the doves flew up from their cypress eyrie. Mark turned, fully expecting to see Beatrice framed in the archway behind him, there to share his concerns. Instead, it was the Mother Superior.

'Sister Concetta told me you intended to come and sit here this afternoon. May I join you?'

'Why, of course, Reverend Mother. I was just reflecting on our talk yesterday evening and considering what I should do next.'

'And have you reached any conclusion?'

'Yes.' He surprised himself by his candour. 'I think I should start to make plans – with your help – to return to England.' In a jaunty, Chevalier-like gesture, he tipped the straw hat to the back of his head, allowing the sun's full force to shine on his face. 'It's been wonderful staying in the convent with you and the sisters, but to remain here longer would, I feel, be something of an indulgence.'

'I see. So would you like me to telephone the travel agency in Syracusa?'

'Yes, please.'

'And you are quite certain, Mark?'

'Yes, Reverend Mother, quite certain.'

VII
Workshop

AT BREAKFAST in the refectory the following morning, Mark found a folded sheet of notepaper in his place at the table. When he opened it, he saw in the Mother Superior's handwriting the details of a flight to Birmingham, which would be departing from the island's Catania airport the following day. She was waiting for him in the hall when he left the refectory.

'Everything is arranged. Our agency says you may pay for your flight at their desk at the airport, and this morning I will ring Georgio in Solarino. He is our local taxi driver and he will drive you to Catania.'

'Thank you, Reverend Mother.'

'I have one more suggestion for you, Mark.'

'Yes?'

'Would you like to try your hand at some light manual labour this morning?'

'Certainly. Am I to go up to the field?'

'No, no, we can't have you getting sunstroke again! I'd like you to go and help Sister Lucia in the workshop with the potpourri. I'm sure you'll find it very interesting and she'll explain how we do it.'

'Where is the workshop?'

She gestured towards the cloisters. 'Go down the right-hand cloister, turn left at the bottom and you'll find the workshop at the far end.'

'But I'm not permitted in the cloisters.'

'I've just given you permission.'

He set off in search of the workshop. It was obvious to see, from this vantage point, why the nuns regarded the cloisters as their private sanctuary. Demarcated by regularly-spaced red sandstone Tuscan columns, the terracotta floor would remain in shade throughout the day. Along the centre of this broad promenade, upturned scallop shells had been set at regular intervals. The artisan who had originally laid these tiles had probably been on the famous *Camino de Santiago* pilgrimage.

The central square which the four sides of the cloisters enclosed was now raked sand, but might once have been a lush greensward, he surmised. At its centre, a simple fountain played: a bronze dolphin discharging water into a circular stone urn. The studded wooden door to the workshop lay at the far end of the second cloister. He knocked and went in. The aroma was almost overpowering.

Sister Lucia was seated at a heavy wooden bench beheading lavender stalks with a pair of sheep shears. An open stook of dried lavender lay scattered in front of her, with several more unopened bundles set on end in the corner. 'Come in, Mark. Come in.'

The little workshop's floor area was no more than three metres square, but the room was lofty. Three of its rough stone walls were vertical, while the fourth was steeply canted, rising to an unglazed circular opening at the top – at least six metres above - through which a bright shaft of sunlight was streaming in. There were a number of old iron hooks driven into the walls and a small triangular fire grate in the corner gave the clue that this room had once been used for smoking hams.

It was a cramped space, given all the paraphernalia stored around the old nun. On a high shelf behind her was a row of tall, unmarked glass jars with gilded necks (probably salvaged from a local apothecary) and to her right was a cardboard box containing dozens of empty crimson sachets with plaited purple cords. In the centre of the workbench was a massive pestle and mortar. The mortar was of turned olive wood and its long pestle had a worn pine handle attached to a pure white carrara marble end.

Lucia put down her shears. 'Would you like me to give you a short tutorial in the ancient Italian art of potpourri?'

'Yes, please.'

'On one condition, though. You must never disclose our formula; it has been kept a secret within the convent for more than two centuries.'

'Of course; I quite understand.'

'I must say, you're very honoured to be sent down here to help me. It's very seldom that Reverend Mother ever lets our guests come in here. Right – on the wall above me are jars with the five principal ingredients which we use: lavender, cinnamon, juniper berries, dried orange peel and nutmeg. Each jar has a wooden ladle inside – all their bowls are a different size, so whatever you do, don't get them mixed up. One level measure of each into this pestle, then crush away to whatever consistency you favour. Some grind it to a powder, while others prefer the potpourri to have a bit of substance. Then you put the mixture into these sachets with this scoop and I will seal their cords with one of these special brass collars.' She took a small ring from her pocket.

'Do you not add any oil?'

'No need. The lavender and juniper berries take care of that.'

'And where do all the filled sachets go? Do you sell them here at the convent?'

'No. Sadly we don't have enough visitors for that. Giorgio from down in the town takes them four times a year to Catania. And from there they're flown to Rome.'

'Rome? I say! Who has them there?'

'The most exclusive perfumery in the city – it's near the Vatican – where they are sold for a great deal of money, I can tell you. So, shall we get started?'

She returned to her lavender shearing, confident that her new apprentice had taken in all her instructions.

They worked on in silence for at least an hour, with the nun occasionally looking up to check that Mark had mastered the technique. When around twenty sachets had been filled, she produced a pair of pliers from her apron, flipped a metal collar around the tightened cord of one of them and crimped it. She handed it to Mark. 'Your wages.'

He turned the filled bag over in his hands, noticing the distinctive aroma was already being exuded though the fabric. The convent's name was printed in gold script on the side of the sachet, with the purple cord's brass collar now bearing an impressed crucifix.

Sister Lucia reached beneath the bench for a large pitcher and poured some lemonade into two wooden beakers. This was clearly a signal for a break. 'So what do you think?'

'I'm impressed.' He sipped the cool fresh lemon drink. 'Tell me, Sister, have you been here at the convent long?'

'I came here first as a novitiate forty-two years ago.'

'Was that by choice?'

'In a manner of speaking. My parents wanted to emigrate to America – my father had been offered a job in a car plant in Detroit – but I didn't want to go. So I suppose you could say it was God's choice that I came here.'

'And have you remained here ever since?'

'Oh yes.' She replaced the jug beneath the bench, but before re-commencing her lavender trimming, reflected wistfully: 'There was one occasion – about six or seven years ago – when Reverend Mother sent three of us to London.'

'Really? What did you do there?'

'We went to represent the convent at your National Gallery's Caravaggio exhibition: we had lent them our Madonna altarpiece.'

'I remember that exhibition well, I went twice.'

'Reverend Mother tells me you've made a special study of the artist.'

'I did, for my dissertation at art college.'

'So you will know then that our Madonna is an earlier version of the one which I believe is in Vienna?'

'Yes, in the *Kunsthistorisches* Museum.'

'By rights, Reverend Mother should have gone to London but of course she wouldn't leave her convent. She is also a Caravaggio expert.'

'Is she?'

'Oh yes, she can tell you so much about the artist. Anyway, I think that's quite enough gossiping. Let us return to our labours!'

Mark carefully measured out another batch of the five ingredients and started grinding. After a while, to break the silence, he asked: 'Do you normally do this work alone?'

'No, one of the other nuns usually comes and gives me a hand, especially when it's coming up to collection time. Little Concetta's my best pupil – she's very fast and always good company.'

'She brought me my breakfast yesterday.'

'Yes, she told me.' The nun smiled ruefully, then after a pause added, without looking up: 'She said she thought you'd seen Beatrice.'

Mark was stunned. So his indiscretion had been picked up by the young nun. He attempted nonchalance. 'Oh really? Why ever would she think that, I wonder?'

'Well, you wouldn't be the first, dear. Concetta has seen her twice, both times in the chapel after Vespers. But then they were very close, those two.'

In an effort to change the subject, Mark finished his drink and glanced across at the lavender stooks standing on the floor. 'Do you grow that yourselves – the lavender?'

'We grow and harvest all the ingredients. So, is it true?'

'Is what true?'

She laid her shears on the bench and looked intently at Mark. 'Did you see her?'

Silently he studied the empty beaker before him.

'Cat got your tongue?'

He looked up at the sympathetically enquiring face of the old nun and nodded, as tears filled his eyes.

VIII
Return to England

THERE WAS no mistaking the arrival of Giorgio's taxi early on Sunday morning. The fifty-year-old, once-red Alfa Romeo Giulietta was clearly in need of a new exhaust and it was probably many years since its bodywork had been washed or polished. Indeed it was a miracle that the driver could even see through the windscreen, such was the thickness of the orange sand which covered it.

The swarthy taxi man bounded across to the gateway where Mark was sheltering in the shade. He handed the cab driver his luggage, then walked back across the courtyard to bid farewell to the Mother Superior and the nine nuns who had all come out to see him off. They had formed two lines on the front steps and he took out his compact camera to snap them, with a beaming Mother Superior standing in the centre at the front.

Mark stowed his camera back in his bag, stepped forward and took both Mother Superior's outstretched hands in his. Then throwing caution to the wind, kissed her on each cheek. She smiled gratefully. 'Look after yourself, Mark. And God bless you.'

And then they were off down the hill, the exhaustless Alfa trumpeting his departure. Mark looked through the raked angle of the taxi's back window just before the outline of the convent disappeared in a cloud of dust, wondering whether Beatrice was watching from his bedroom window.

Giorgio was initially taciturn, observing his passenger suspiciously though the rear view mirror, though once they'd reached the main autoroute leading north he relaxed a little. The Alfa's interior had been as neglected as its bodywork, with most of the original black leather upholstery split or missing. The uncovered parts of the seat squab Mark was sitting on exuded the familiar orange and cinnamon aroma of the convent's potpourri. He was sharing the rear seat with a large sack of lemons.

'Sister Lucia was telling me about the consignments of their potpourri which you take to the airport.'

'Si, signore.'

'And it goes all the way to Rome, I believe?'

'Si, signore.'

'I greatly enjoyed my stay with the nuns. They are most hospitable.'

'Si, signore.'

'Have you worked for them long?'

'*Si, signore*, many years. Once my daughter was a nun at the convent.'

'Really? But no longer?'

'No *signore*. No longer.'

'Where is she now?'

'In Heaven, I hope, *signore*. She died two years ago.'

There was no need for Mark to ask Georgio the name of his daughter and for the remainder of the journey to Catania airport he decided it was prudent to study the beautiful Sicilian countryside in silence. He reflected on the curious irony of being driven away from his 'lover' by her father.

Mark's month in Sicily had passed all too quickly. Though he felt rested, and believed that the anxieties caused by his lost job, and the break-up with his partner were behind him, he wondered whether a new and more emotionally-troubling prospect had appeared to replace them.

Catania was small, crowded and stiflingly hot. After settling up with Giorgio, Mark quickly located the local travel agency where all his ticketing arrangements had been efficiently taken care of. After a tedious wait in an overcrowded departures lounge, the UK-bound passengers were shepherded across the tarmac to their waiting easyJet aeroplane and within half-an-hour were airborne.

Mark asked to be re-seated in the back row, in order to get as far away as possible from a group of hungover hen party celebrants. Then, declining offers of food and drink, he slept for most of the journey back to England.

The plane's touch-down and its passengers' speedy movement through UK immigration and customs meant that Mark just had time to dash across to the airport's train station to catch the last train to London. Less than three hours after arriving back in England, he was standing in the concourse of a near-deserted Euston Station. It was shortly before midnight.

He stepped outside into the cool night air. Many dossers had already taken up their positions on benches, submerged beneath layers of blankets or old duvets or newspapers. A line of black cabs stood waiting at the station terminus's official rank, though there were no customers at this hour. Fifty yards away, alongside a bus stop, was a bright orange Skoda mini-cab, with its Pakistani driver reading a newspaper. As Mark strolled up, he lowered his window. 'Where to, mate?'

'I'm not certain. I need to find some overnight accommodation.'

He dropped his newspaper onto the passenger seat. 'Well, if we go south from here, there's Bloomsbury – you know, where the British Museum is? Lots of hotels around there will take you in at this hour. Or east of here (he pointed through the cab's windscreen), just down the Euston Road, there's a Novotel, which they say is cheap and clean.' He retrieved his newspaper and began folding it as if to begin reading again. 'Personally, if I was you and wanted to save meself the price of the taxi fare, I'd walk round the back of this station and try the Travellers Rest hostel first.'

'I might do that. Thanks.'

As Mark stepped back onto the pavement to pick up his luggage, he glanced at the sign on the mini-cab's door. Above a telephone number it read 'KazCabs'.

'Tell me: your mini-cab company, KazCabs... is the boss man's name Kasmin, by any chance?'

'That's right, mate.'

'Turkish guy?'

'I believe so.'

'About my age?'

The driver looked him up and down. 'Yup, I'd say so. Why d'you ask?'

'Only that I think I was at art college with your boss. Small world, isn't it? Anyway thanks for the hostel tip, I'll go and give it a try.'

Memorising the taxi firm's telephone number, Mark shouldered his bag and set off to find the Travellers Rest.

The Euston Square Travellers Rest hostel was bright and welcoming, although the Nigerian night receptionist seemed slightly put out to have been awoken after midnight. 'I'll have to charge you the full rate, even though it's the middle of the night,' he said pointedly.

'Fine. Make it two nights. I'll be checking out on Tuesday.'

'How are you paying?'

'Visa?' Mark passed his card across the glass counter and the receptionist turned it over in his hand several times as if it was contaminated.

'Is there a problem?'

'Dunno 'til I put it through.' The electronic transaction went through without a hitch and Mark put his credit card back in his wallet. He was handed a plastic room pass. 'Eight eleven; eighth floor. Lift's in the corner.'

'And breakfast?'

'Self-service from 6 a.m., but it's extra and we don't do cooked dishes.'

The perfunctory exchanges having been concluded, Mark walked across the lobby to the lift to leave the surly Nigerian to resume his nap.

Room 811 was not so much a bedroom as a minimalist sleeping cell with adjoining washroom. A full-length hessian curtain screened the window and the double bed was covered by a single sheet and a thin duvet. The mini-bar was empty. Mark didn't bother to undress and just stretched out on top of the bed and was soon asleep.

He awoke at 9 a.m. and took a shower in the pod-like washroom. After two cups of instant coffee he put in a call to the minicab company whose number he had noted outside Euston Station.

'Good morning, KazCabs. How may I help you?'

'Oh, good morning. I was wondering if I might have a word with your proprietor, Kasmin? I'm an old friend.'

'Who shall I say is calling?'

'Tell him it's Mark, Mark Sutton.'

'Hold the line a moment.'

The 'moment' turned into three or four minutes of Turkish music, before the lady receptionist came back on the line. 'He doesn't seem to be answering. Can you call back?'

'Sure. How long shall I leave it?'

'I should try again after 11 a.m.'

Mark's second telephone call from his bedroom was more fruitful. His eighty-year-old paternal grandmother – known always as Granny Sutton – was delighted to hear his voice.

'Mark! How nice to hear you – are you still in Italy?'

'Sicily. No Gran, I'm back in London. Arrived late last night.'

He picked up the phone cradle and walked over to the window to look at the view northwards across London.

'I only got your card this morning and it never said anything about coming back.'

'It was a bit of a spur of the moment decision, Gran. I'd had a nice rest and decided it was time I got back to civilisation.'

'And whereabouts are you ringing from?'

'Euston Square.'

'Sounds very posh.'

'I can assure you it isn't! It's a sort of hostel, although the one bonus is the view from my bedroom window – looking north up to Hampstead Heath. I bet if I looked really hard, I could see your block of flats in Kentish Town. What floor are you on?'

'The sixth floor, dear.'

'This room's on the eighth.'

'Well I never. So you enjoyed yourself, did you, Mark?'

'Yes, I did.' Staring across the parallel rail tracks flowing into Euston, St Pancras and King's Cross, he momentarily wondered what had possessed him to exchange the tranquil views from his bedroom window in the convent for this dreary urban landscape.

'And when am I going to hear all about it – this convent you've been staying in?'

'That's one of the reasons why I'm ringing, Gran. You know all that stuff I left with you?'

'Don't worry dear, it's all quite safe. It's in the spare room just where you left it.'

'It's principally my computer I need. I was wondering if I could pop over some time to pick it up?'

'Of course. When were you thinking?'

'Can't manage today. I've got to make contact with an old mate. Towards the end of the week, perhaps?'

'I know: why not come for Sunday lunch? I could do one of my special roasts. You like those.'

'Hey, that would be wonderful, Gran. What time shall I come?'

'Well, I like to go to church with Miss Hawkins from next door, so why don't we say around midday?'

'Perfect! Twelve o'clock on Sunday. See you then.'

'I'll look forward to it, dear. Goodbye.'

After he rang off, Mark finished dressing and decided to give the hostel's self-service breakfast bar a miss. Instead, he set forth to try to find a decent café which served hot meals. Outside the entrance, a veritable tidal wave of office workers was flowing past, most clutching cardboard mugs of cappuccino and rolled-up copies of *Metro*. They all looked equally glum.

By-passing a clutch of espresso bars with long queues, he happened upon what he decided had to be one of Euston's last-surviving 'greasy spoons'. He went in to order his first full English for a month.

The interior could have been a 1950s railway station waiting room, its white distempered walls decorated with out-of-date speedway and professional wrestling posters. The intense humidity was overlaid with a smell of grilled bacon fat and brown sauce. The clientele was made up largely of cab drivers and parking wardens, most of whom were reading *The Sun*.

Clad in a soiled apron - which had once upon a time been white – a swarthy-looking wall-eyed Greek proprietor held court. He bore more than a passing resemblance to The Mighty Cyclops in one of the 20-year-old wrestling posters. Mark's order was bellowed through a small hatch: 'One full English, no black pudding!'

The cooked breakfast, when it finally arrived, was average but its presentation and service were abominable. He recalled the theatricality of the beautiful barista in the café near the square in Solarino. Looking around at this London café's doleful customers, he once more wondered what had possessed him to leave Sicily.

Back in his room at the Travellers Rest, Mark made a second attempt to reach Kasmin.

'Mark? Mark Sutton – is it really you, you old bastard?'

'It certainly is. And am I really addressing the owner of a fleet of London mini-cabs?'

'It's not all it's cracked up to be, mate, believe you me. You should see my fucking overdraft. Where are you calling from?'

'Euston Square.'

'I thought you were running a posh art gallery in Belsize Park?'

'I was, but not any longer. It folded.'

'No? I'm sorry mate. And how's the lovely Maggie?'

'Gone. That, I'm afraid, folded too.'

'Shame.'

'You? How's Dee?'

'Dee and I are no longer an item, as they say.'

The line went silent, while the two men mentally absorbed these dramatic changes to their personal lives.

'Mark – we've gotta meet up, mate. Why don't you come over here and we'll take a bevy or two at the local?'

'Where's here?'

'King's Cross. Behind the station.'

'OK. When?'

'Later today?'

'Fine.'

'Say around five?'

'Perfect. How do I find you?'

'Got internet access?'

'Not at the moment.'

'Right. Head for the McDonalds on Caledonian Road, then take the second right. KazCabs's office is next door to the betting shop.'

'Got it. I'll see you later!'

'Look forward to it.'

Mark had already made a mental note while eating his breakfast that the next item on his agenda had to be to find himself somewhere to live, since being holed up in a small room on the eighth floor of a second-rate hostel, he had decided, would pretty quickly drive him crazy.

He flicked through the copy of *Metro* he'd picked up in the hostel's lobby and noted a couple of estate agents' addresses in Bloomsbury, then got ready to go out.

Once he'd shaken off the noise and exhaust pollution of the Euston

Road and headed southwards, the quieter, leafy streets of Bloomsbury had a calming effect. The huge Corinthian columns of the British Museum hove into view and he veered eastwards in the direction of Brunswick Square, where the first agency was located.

'I can offer you a very nice studio apartment in a mansion block off Russell Square for £650 a calendar month. We've got the keys here if you'd like to view it,' said the receptionist. 'Otherwise, I'm afraid I've got nothing under £1k in the locality you're after. Bloomsbury's extremely popular at the moment, sir.'

A rent of £1,000, Mark decided, was about as much as he'd be willing to pay for a flat for three months, let alone one. He beat a discreet retreat, declining to leave his e-mail address for 'regular property updates'.

After checking the window display of the second estate agent, he realised that Bloomsbury was not only 'extremely popular' but way beyond his means. His share of the Belsize Park flat, which he and Maggie had owned and sold, would soon be swallowed up.

Lunch came next and he took a seat under a sun umbrella outside a quiet Italian *trattoria* in the pedestrianised square. The waitress who brought him the menu said she would enquire whether they had any Sicilian wines and triumphantly reappeared bearing a bottle of Nero d'Avola, which she held before him. Its rich fruity lustre brought back wonderful memories of the island. The young woman returned to take his pizza order and re-fill his glass. Mark decided that his flat-hunting should be abandoned for the day, and instead he would visit the British Museum, before heading down to King's Cross.

The Caledonian Road was as grim and dirty as he remembered it – an ancient cattle drovers' highway into London which, for two centuries, 'gentrification' had passed by. The McDonalds was an easy landmark to spot and the second side turning was as depressing as the main road. Beyond a betting shop there was a narrow alleyway littered with empty beer cans, used condoms and a bicycle pedal. At the far end, KazCabs' offices looked no bigger than a seaside chalet. He entered a tiny outer office, at which an attractive young Pakistani woman – no more than twenty, Mark guessed – was talking via a head mic to a taxi driver.

'No, Geoff, I didn't say Mornington Terrace, you berk, I said Mornington Crescent; I've got it written down here! Number 36. She's a regular, and she's furious – been on three times already.'

'Take me a good ten minutes to get over there, Dina.'

'Well get a move on!'

'Wilco.'

The taxi despatcher looked up. 'Need a cab?'

'No. Actually, I've called to see Kasmin if he's in? I'm an old friend. He told me to call by at around five.'

'You rang earlier? You must be Mark. I'm Dina.'

'Hello.'

She flicked a switch on the console beside her computer keyboard. 'Kaz – Mark's here.'

The half-glazed door of the 'chalet's' inner office was swung open to reveal a beaming, dark-skinned, clean-shaven man, with swept-back black hair. He wore an expensive, branded casual top and tight-fitting grey chinos. 'Mark!' he barked, stepping forward with arms outstretched. 'You old bastard! How are you?' He enveloped Mark in a huge bear hug, from which Mark had to quickly disengage, due to Kasmin's overpowering aftershave.

'I'm good.' He felt his response was delivered without conviction, so he repeated it more affirmatively. 'Yes. I'm good. And you? I can't get over this new-found entrepreneurship. You used to despise capitalism.'

'I know, I know. If you can't beat 'em – and we sure as hell never will – then join 'em.'

Suddenly realising that Dina had been silently witnessing this reunion, Kasmin looked down at her and snatched up one of her hands. The diamond-encrusted Rolex was hard to ignore. 'And did you meet my lovely Dina? This young woman is the love of my life.'

Mark nodded shyly. 'Yes, we said hello.'

Kasmin leant forward and kissed her forehead. 'Me and Mark are going round the corner for a bevy or two in the Granby. Can I leave you in charge, darling?'

'Sure, Kaz.'

Just as the two old mates were about to depart for the pub, with Kasmin's arm around Mark's shoulder, the taxi-intercom sprang into life with a crackle.

'Dina? There ain't no Mornington Parade, darling.'

Looking up at Kasmin in sheer frustration, she bawled into the mic: 'Crescent! Crescent, you dickhead!'

'Sorry, I thought you said Parade. Right, Crescent. Mornington Crescent – 63 wasn't it?'

'No! 36. It's 36 Mornington Crescent. Gotta go, I've got an incomer – and no fucking guesses who it's gonna be!' She deftly switched across to the in-coming call, as Mark and Kasmin hovered in the doorway. 'Mrs Lieberman. Yes, yes, I know. My driver tells me he'll be with you inside five minutes. Traffic's horrendous, he says. There's been a most terrible accident in Piccadilly – busload of schoolgirls, I believe. Oh, has he; outside now? Lovely. There you are, Mrs Lieberman – KazCabs always delivers!'

She clicked the switch, looked up at the two men frozen in the doorway and winked. 'Enjoy!'

Mark and Kasmin left. Then the mini-cab proprietor went back. 'Cards and money, Dina; blow that wanker out!'

Kasmin's local hostelry, The Marquis of Granby, turned out to be something of a time-warp: a heavily-ornate Victorian pub with many of its 150-year-old fixtures still intact. The giant mirror behind the bar advertised a beer which had been extinct for almost a century, and the acid-etched glass windows onto the street depicted a crinoline-clad lady descending from a horse-drawn hansom cab.

Kasmin planted the two pint glasses of lager onto the corner table and sat down opposite Mark, who was seated on a crimson-buttoned banquette.

'So what were you doing in Sicily?'

'Chilling out. Recuperating.'

'From the split-up with Maggie?'

Mark nodded and sipped his beer. 'And the gallery folding.'

'So how did that happen? I thought that couple who owned it had got the art world sussed. And Belsize Park's a superb location.'

'I know, Kaz. But we were offered a Freud...'

'Lucien?'

'Allegedly.'

'And?'

'And they didn't check the provenance!'

Kasmin took a long gulp of lager. 'Don't tell me!'

'It was brought in by this scruffy-looking, overweight Jamaican woman who claimed she'd been his cleaning lady.'

'What was the picture of?'

'Her. Nude. Sat on a wicker chair wearing green wellies! Eighteen inches square: his favourite size for small pieces. It was incredibly convincing. It had me fooled, I can tell you, and I'd followed his work for more than ten years. The brushwork was immaculate.'

'And they bought it off her?'

Mark nodded and finished his lager. 'I know: they should've offered to sell it for her on commission, but they suddenly got greedy.'

'How much?'

'Sixty thousand.'

'Fucking hell. How naive can you get? And it's worth?'

Mark shrugged. 'Probably the price of the canvas – a fiver.'

'Goodbye Belsize Arts?'

'Exactly; within a fortnight. They'd taken out a hefty great high-interest short-term bank loan. Three days later, Maggie announced that she'd been having an affair with her psychotherapist.'

'Double-bummer.'

'Triple-bummer.'

'How come?'

'The psychotherapist is a woman.' Mark got up and went to the bar for refills.

When he returned, he decided that he needed to discover more about Kasmin's love life. 'So Dina – how did that come about, you old dog?'

Kasmin took a swig. 'After Alice came along, Dee lost interest in sex. Sad. But it sometimes happens, especially with western women. Turkish women are different. I was down here every day from seven in the morning until late. And Dina was running an incredibly tight ship – we've got twelve cars out most days. And, well, we just sort of clicked, as you might say. She's amazing, mate, in every department.'

'Well, you certainly seem very happy. So what about Deirdre? What happened there?'

'She's still in the house – you remember, the one up in Caroline Square? Alice is 16 now. Waiting to go to college – though I couldn't get her into Saint Martin's, like us.'

'And has Dee found anyone else?'

'Nah!'

'And the mini-cabbing business is OK?'

'Fair to middling. Yes, I suppose we're doing OK. Just wait 'til the Granary Square development is finished – that's all those office blocks they're putting up behind the station – it's gonna make a huge difference, especially when Google arrives!'

The adjoining table in the quiet snug they'd secured had been taken by a smartly-suited man, who parked a voluminous holdall under the banquette. His facial appearance was arresting, Mark decided. Could he be wearing make-up? The cheeks were too pink; the eyebrows were too black; and his lips were positively ruby red.

'Sorry, Kaz, what was that?'

'I asked if you'd found anyone? A love of your life, perhaps?'

An unexpected low blow, which winged him for a moment. Mark hadn't thought about Beatrice for two days. 'Yes and no.'

'Meaning?'

'Meaning, I did meet someone in Sicily, but it didn't work out. Simple as that.'

'Would you gentlemen mind keeping an eye on my bag – here under the chair - while I just freshen up my glass?' asked their neighbour.

'Sure,' they answered in unison.

The man returned, bearing a huge cocktail in a coaster.

Mark nodded at him. 'That looks interesting.'

'Mojito.'

'Come again?'

'Mojito. It's the national drink of Cuba.'

'Is that a fact?'

'White rum, sugar syrup, lime juice, crushed mint leaves, soda and ice. Like to try?' He offered his glass to Mark.

Mark hesitated as Kasmin looked on with interest. He accepted the offer and took a sip.

'Mmmm. Tasty.'

'Me or the cocktail?'

'The mojito. I could get addicted to that very easily.'

Kasmin crashed into the flirtatious dialogue. 'Mark, I'd better be getting back in case Dina's had problems with Geoff. Listen, this place you're staying in up at Euston: how long are you gonna be there?'

'Few more days. Just until I find somewhere to rent.'

'Any prospects?'

'Not at the moment. I took a look at Bloomsbury this morning but it's way beyond my reach.'

'Only, it's just...I was thinking. Dee – my ex – has got a couple of rooms in the basement of our old house round the corner. And she's been talking about renting them out. Would you like me to sound her out to see if she's still looking for a tenant?'

'Hey, Kaz that would be brilliant!'

'Right. Pop round to the office in half an hour or so and I'll try to find out if she might be interested. In the meantime,' he winked and nodded his head sideways, 'have fun!'

Mark suddenly felt stranded. It was obvious that Kasmin wanted to get back to bill and coo with his dusky-eyed Pakistani lover. He'd finished his lager and decided he'd have one more drink. He looked across at his 'neighbour', whose eyelashes now seemed to have grown half-inch extensions.

'Err...would you like another?'

'Thanks, sweetie that would be divine.' The empty glass was handed across.

Waiting to be served at the bar, Mark spotted a poster advertising a Drag Karaoke night. He wandered back, handed the stranger the new drink and settled on the bench beside him.

'That's a gorgeous tan you've got there. Where did that come from?'

'Sicily.'

'Nice.'

They sipped their mojitos simultaneously. 'And are you competing in the karaoke tonight?'

'Hope to – if I'm not legless. Got my outfit in this bag underneath.'

'And what number do you sing to?'

'Big Spender. The Shirley McLaine show-stopper?'

'I'd like to see it.'

'Why not come along, darling?'

'What's your name?'

'Linda.'

'OK, I might do that, Linda'. Leaving a suitable pause so that it didn't appear as a snub, Mark finished his cocktail and stood up. 'Must fly. May see you later.'

'I hope so.'

KazCabs' outer office was calmer, with Dina engrossed in a copy of *Hello*. Kasmin appeared from his inner sanctum without being summoned. 'Yup, fine. It's all set up, mate. Dee says if you'd like to call at the house tomorrow around 11 a.m. she'll show you the two basement rooms. But don't expect luxury – the last time I saw them they were full of junk!'

Mark shook his head. 'Don't worry, Kaz, right now anything would be better than solitary confinement in my Euston Square hostel!'

Kasmin handed him a KazCabs card, on the back of which he'd written Deirdre's address and telephone number, with a simple directional map.

Mark walked back down the Caledonian Road, intending to pick up a bus back to the hostel from outside King's Cross station. While he was waiting he flipped Kasmin's card over and saw that, by making a simple zig-zag detour, he could pass across the bottom of Caroline Square, then walk back to Euston.

It was certainly worth the extra shoe leather. Caroline Square was technically in Somers Town, though the German Luftwaffe had erased most of the district's early-Georgian tenement blocks. London's road planners hadn't yet discovered this enclave and so its grid street pattern, culminating at Caroline Square, was largely intact. It was a handsome civic space, with unbroken terraces of Georgian town houses on all four sides, overlooking an oval park ringed by railings. He stood in the corner he had entered by, in order to get his bearings. If the house numbering was logical, he figured number 25 had to be somewhere in the centre of the top-most terrace. He crossed over to the central park, in which a mother and two toddlers were playing. A sign saying 'Residents Only' warned him against entering.

The square's northernmost terrace was by far the most impressive, with its dozen or so south-facing three-storey houses all looking well maintained and tidy. Number 25 had uncovered brickwork at basement and ground floor levels, then white stucco reaching to a parapet in front of a slate roof. There were lights burning in all the front rooms. On the top floor, a young woman was sitting at the window reading a magazine with headphones on. Below, in a lofty first-floor room, an older woman was ironing. The long ground floor room was empty, but it was easy to work out that it ran the full depth of the house. Its all-white décor and sparse furnishings bore the hallmarks of a day's shopping at either IKEA or Habitat.

Having completed his stealthy reconnaissance, Mark headed back to Euston Square, well pleased with what he'd seen.

IX

Dee and Alice

THE NEXT morning, Mark was awoken at six o'clock by slanting squalls of rain being dashed against his bedroom window. It was just light, but a dull, depressing grey light, the sort of prospect which makes one want to scurry back to the still-warm bed and hide beneath the bedclothes. But in the Euston Square Travellers Rest, traditional bedclothes were considered an anachronism.

Mark slouched around his room, wearing the duvet as a dressing gown 'cloak', while the contents of the slow-witted electric kettle roused itself sufficiently to infuse an unmarked sachet of instant coffee chips into something which would have to pass as a cup of coffee. And the mug was chipped. An hour later, showered and sufficiently spruced up for pounding the London pavements, he rode down to the hostel's lobby.

He was relieved to find that the sullen Nigerian had been replaced by an attractive Eastern European lady receptionist. She assured him that extending his stay by two more nights in the same bedroom was 'not a problem at all.' She didn't even ask to see his Visa card.

In his waterproof top, he waited under Euston Station's canopy for a bus which would take him down to the Caledonian Road to meet Kaz's ex-wife Deirdre at her house on Caroline Square.

The rain was easing as he alighted in front of the new-look King's Cross station, reformed out of all recognition. Office workers were streaming out, ignoring a line of persistent God-botherers strung out across the pedestrian precinct. Mark decided to walk up to take a look at the Granary Wharf development which Kasmin had mentioned, before dropping down to the Georgian square from the opposite direction he'd approached it the evening before.

He purchased a chocolate pastry and a cappuccino from a trolley outside the main line station and walked northwards up the long, traffic-free hill. Behind the huge advertising hoardings which flanked the route, office towers in various states of structural completion were rising up on huge building sites. The few that were finished – though still unoccupied – indicated that this development was destined to become a scaled-down version of London's Canary Wharf financial quarter. Kasmin's confident prediction that Google's arrival would bring prosperity to the area seemed prescient.

Granary Wharf itself was a total contrast. A huge, five-storey Victorian warehouse overshadowed a broad, paved square – easily the size of a football pitch – with an elaborate, multi-jetted water feature at its centre. He took a seat on one of the stone benches to finish his coffee and study this man-made civic space.

Clutches of students entering the warehouse indicated that it must contain an educational facility and on closer inspection, Mark was pleasantly surprised to discover that this was now the new home of his old art college of Saint Martin's, which had once been based in Covent Garden.

Inside, he spent a good hour absorbed by an exhibition of students' work set around the central lobby, before leaving to head for Caroline Square.

By day, bathed by morning sunlight, No 25 looked even more attractive. He stood on the tiled front porch and rang the bell. After a long pause, followed by footsteps hastily descending a staircase, the door was swung open by an attractive dark-haired woman in her early forties. She wore a plain white T-shirt under the braces of a pair of blue denim dungarees. The low-cut line of the bib left little doubt that she wasn't wearing a bra.

She smiled in recognition. 'Hi Mark! How are you?'

'Hi Dee! I'm good.'

'Come on in.'

He followed her into the uncarpeted hall, down which he glimpsed a view of a long garden, through a half-open door.

'How long has it been?' asked Dee over her shoulder as she led him into the all-white living room he'd seen the night before.

'Ten years?'

'Must be.'

'Kaz tells me you and Maggie split up.' She gestured to a Chesterfield sofa. A modern jazz CD was playing through two huge speakers at the far end of the room.

'Yeah, 'fraid so. And I expect he told you the art gallery went pear-shaped around the same time?'

Deirdre perched on the arm of an armchair. 'Yes – rotten luck all round for you. Can I get you a drink? Tea, coffee?'

'I wouldn't mind a glass of water, Dee.'

She jumped up and went to the back of the living space, which was a fully-equipped open-plan kitchen, taking a jug of chilled water from a huge, American-style refrigerator.

She returned with the jug and two tumblers. 'And nowhere to live?'

'Nope. I sniffed around Bloomsbury a bit yesterday, but to tell you the truth I was shocked at the rents they were quoting.'

'Tell me about it!' She poured his drink.

'What's going on?'

'Foreign investors is the polite explanation. But I'd say it's more like ex-pats – Libyan, Egyptian, Syrian even – finding somewhere to stuff their money out of harm's way.' She sat in the armchair and crossed her legs. 'So where else have you looked?'

'Nowhere yet. I thought I might try Camden Town later.'

'Grotty old Camden? Well you might have some luck there, but if it's within walking distance of Regent's Park, you can forget it!'

The jazz music – dominated by a hauntingly beautiful piano solo – washed over him.

'Anyway, do you want to have a look at the rooms downstairs? I should warn you, it's not a flat in the strict sense of the word. At the moment it's just a couple of basement rooms full of junk, much of it left behind by my dear ex-husband!'

She took his water glass and returned it to the kitchen. He followed her through in order to take a peep at the garden. Half-way down a lawned area, a young girl was sunbathing face down on a striped sun lounger, wearing only the bottom half of a bikini. Her cropped, bleached-blonde haircut had a violent pink streak down its centre.

They went back into the hall where Dee unbolted a narrow panelled door under the staircase. She switched on a light and cautiously led the way below.

'Now be very careful, Mark: the treads of these stairs are extremely narrow and there are one or two wonky ones.'

'OK, I'll watch out. You lead on.'

They descended in silence, one step at a time. At the bottom, she unlatched another narrow panelled door, flicked on a second light and stepped into the basement space. Mark followed, almost losing his balance on a loose stair edge near the bottom.

'Excuse the smell; it's just that we have to keep the front window locked for security reasons.'

She walked across between the debris to unfasten and open a big sash window. The natural light flooding in revealed two large mattresses, a child's push bike, a rusty twin-tub washing machine, a striped sun lounger, strung-up bundles of magazines and sundry cardboard boxes overflowing with papers.

She looked down at the boxes contemptuously. 'Most of this rubbish is Kaz's. I've lost count of the number of times I've asked him to shift it.' She moved forwards. 'Right, then through here is the back room.' She unlocked a connecting door and passed through to a room of similar size at the back of the house. Here there was slightly less detritus, though the musty odour lingered. An old-fashioned glazed sink with a white enamel draining board was in the far corner. Set into the ceiling at the far end was a dusty skylight.

'When we bought the place, our architect tried to persuade us to make this the kitchen. But I'm glad we didn't; I like my kitchen upstairs, where I can see the garden'.

'Any toilet arrangements down here?' Mark asked.

'Very primitive, I'm afraid. In fact positively Victorian!'

She led the way back across the front half of the basement, then unlocked a barred and bolted outside door. Beyond was an open outside cellar area, with stone steps leading up to the street. Dee stood outside, while Mark remained in the doorway.

'The good news is you've got your own entrance – once we get a proper Yale lock fitted to that door. The bad news is that this is your loo!' She gestured theatrically with one hand.

The small cubbyhole alongside the coal cellar was, as she'd described, positively Victorian, with a chain-operated high-level cistern and a toilet bowl with a wooden seat. He took a look inside, then she pulled the toilet door shut and followed Mark back into the front room, bolting the outside entrance door.

With arms on hips, she looked at him plaintively. 'Well, what do you think?'

Mark surveyed all the junk, then stepped up to the window and looked up at the railings on the street. He sauntered back to take a second look at the back half. He was already trying to furnish the two linked spaces in his head. 'It's certainly got potential, Dee. And I imagine that if you got a competent builder in and spent, say, two or three thousand modernising it, you'd have yourself a nice little earner. For which I expect a local estate agent could quickly conjure up a tenant for you who'd be willing to pay – oh, I don't know – £300 a week?'

She nodded but let him continue to ruminate.

'But my needs are rather simpler – and more immediate. I dare say we could get rid of Kaz's rubbish in a morning, then both rooms want properly cleaning and decorating.'

'And there's the problem of no shower?'

'Yes. But I'm not too worried about the antique loo.'

'That's a relief! I was dreading having to show you that. Let's go back upstairs, shall we?'

'Sure.'

'Shall I make us a *cafetière* of coffee?' she asked pleasantly, as she washed her hands in the kitchen sink.

'That would be nice. Thanks.'

She hit one of the CD player's buttons and the crisp, tinkling piano music began again.

'By the way, I love your choice of music – so calming. Who is it?'

'EST.'

'Say again?'

'The Esbjörn Svensson Trio. They're Swedish.' She passed him the CD's cover, which showed three young men looking earnestly at the camera. The title was 'Seven Days of Falling.'

'I'd love to hear them live in a concert hall.'

She placed a mug of coffee on the table beside him, with a small jug of milk and a glass of water. 'I'm afraid that won't be possible.'

'Why not? Don't they come to the UK?'

'Esbjörn Svensson's dead. He died in a scuba-diving accident. He was only forty-four.'

'When was this?'

'Two years ago.'

Accompanied by the plaintive piano solo that was playing from the speaker beside him, Dee's last words had almost the same effect on Mark as the Mother Superior's words in the convent. They drank their coffee in silence.

'Listen, Dee, I like your basement rooms very much and I think I could do something with them for you. The number one problem, it seems to me, is getting rid of all Kaz's crap. Would the bin men take any of it?'

'The small stuff, maybe – if it's bagged up. But they're a pretty stroppy lot around here. This is the Soviet Republic of Camden, after all!'

'Skip hire?'

'Very expensive and if you don't stand guard over 'em all night, they're full to overflowing by the next morning!'

'Really?'

'Somers Town skip-dumping is legendary.'

'Well how would it be if I had a word with Kaz?'

'You could try,' she said half-heartedly, pulling a face.

'He's been ignoring all your requests, but if I tried the 'old mates' line, you never know, he might play ball.'

'No harm in trying. Why not give him a ring now?'

'OK.' She went into the hall and brought back a cordless handset.

Mark pulled the KazCabs card from his top pocket and tapped in the number.

'Good afternoon, KazCabs. How may I help you?'

'Hi Dina – it's Mark Sutton. I called to see Kasmin yesterday. Could I have a quick word with him?'

'He's just popped out for some ciggies, Mark. Shall I get him to call you back?'

'Yes please. Tell him I'm at Dee's.'

'Will do. Bye.'

Mark stood up to stretch his legs and return the mug to the kitchen worktop. The garden was now in full sun and the young sunbather had turned onto her back on the sun lounger and was tapping out text messages on her pink iPhone. Her small, perfectly-formed breasts were on view for all to see.

Coming into the kitchen, Dee said apologetically: 'That's Alice. I'm afraid my daughter is utterly shameless. It's partly because we've become accustomed to living in a man-free environment – she walks around the house with nothing on half the time – but out there I think she sometimes does it to wind up our elderly neighbours!' She rinsed the mugs and chuckled. 'A couple of weeks back, we had a mini-heat wave. Alice was out there starkers: on her back, knees bent, legs open! I quite expected to hear an ambulance siren outside as they collected a coronary collapse from one of the flats down the street!'

At that moment the phone rang. Dee answered it, passing it across to Mark without speaking, silently mouthing 'Kaz'.

'Hi Kasmin.'

'So what d'you think of the basement?'

'It's difficult to see the wood for the trees just at the moment, mate!' Dee smirked.

'How d'you mean?'

'All your drossy crap. It's only fit for the skip.'

'I know, I know. Give it the heave-ho, mate. I've no objections. So, do I take it you might be moving in?'

'Don't know. Too early to say.' Looking across to Dee, he added: 'We haven't even discussed terms. But I'll get back to you if we need a hand with transport.'

'Sure. Be glad to help.'

The call ended, Mark handed Dee the phone back. 'Well done, Mark. I've never managed that. It's always: "There's lots of important KazCabs records down there I need to sort through". The wally!'

Now back in both halves of her bikini, Alice suddenly appeared in the kitchen, still texting with two thumbs.

'Alice, this is Mark, an old friend of dad's.'

'Hi.' She didn't look up.

'Would you like to stay for a bite to eat, Mark?' Dee asked. 'Alice could pop round to The Daffodil and get us some stuffed vine leaves and pitta breads. Eh, Alice?'

'Cool. I'll go and put some clothes on.' She slouched out, still texting.

'That's kind of you, Dee. Maybe this afternoon we could make a start downstairs?'

'If you like.'

Dee took a bottle of retsina from the fridge and held it up. 'Would you like a glass? I'm going to have a spritzer.'

'Thanks. About the rent for the rooms downstairs – if I was going to rent them from you. Do you have any ideas?'

'I haven't a clue, sweetie.' The 'sweetie' seemed to pop out involuntarily and she looked away quickly. 'You say a figure because I hate haggling.'

'Well, like we said earlier, with a full-blown makeover you'd have no problems getting £300 a week.'

'Yes, I know. But that's with tenancy agreements and references and a huge wedge for the agent's commission. I was thinking more of an informal arrangement, if you know what I mean? You as our downstairs lodger? Cash in hand?'

'Absolutely. Well, if I offered to decorate it out for you and bring in my own furniture, how would £150 a week seem to you?'

'Too much. If you're going to help me get rid of Kaz's crap, I'd be happy with £100.'

'Are you sure?'

'Positive. Let's drink to it, shall we?' They raised their glasses as Alice re-appeared, wearing an ultra-short tennis skirt and a One Direction T-shirt. 'Money?'

Dee took her handbag from a kitchen shelf and fished out a £20 note. 'Three stuffed vine leaves, three pitta breads and get us another bottle of this white, would you, darling?'

'Cool.' Alice padded off in her flip-flops and Dee re-filled their wine glasses.

A quarter of an hour later, the front door slammed shut. Alice stood beaming in the sitting room doorway, clutching a large brown paper carrier. 'Skip ahoy!'

Mark looked on bemused. These two women, separated by about twenty-five years, were like two peas in a man-free pod. Was this some private argot?

'Skip?' asked a wide-eyed Dee. 'Where?'

'Round the corner in Keir Hardie Street. Just arrived. I watched them unloading it in front of that cleared building site.' Then she added, spreading her arms wide for dramatic effect, still clutching the carrier: 'Fucking massive, it is, really, really huge!'

'Language, Alice.' Dee turned to Mark. 'Looks like it could be our lucky day. What say we have a quick bite to eat and then go and check it out? Wouldn't it be absolutely brilliant if we could get shot of those mattresses and the washing machine and Alice's old bike?'

An hour later (having finished the bottle of retsina), they set off to inspect Alice's skip, but the Somers Town skip-dumpers had already been out. Atop a mini-mountain of bulging supermarket carrier bags towered a purple and crimson uncut moquette sofa. On tip-toe, Alice peered over the skip's side. 'Might get my bike in, but that's about it.'

Two youths appeared around the corner carrying a moth-eaten armchair. Dejectedly, the trio retraced their steps to 25 Caroline Square.

'It's all *your* fault!' Alice snapped at Dee.

'How come?'

'Because if we'd gone out as soon as I'd told you about the skip and *then* had our food, we would have got rid of most of that poxy junk from the basement!'

Dee's raised eyebrows gave Mark a 'She's right, you know' look. She continued brewing the tea, which they drank at the kitchen table.

Mark decided to take the lead.

'Listen guys: I've got a plan. We go back, wheeling the twin tub? Then Alice uses it as a sort of ladder to get up into the skip and sort of rearrange things a bit – so we can slide the two mattresses in. Possibly even her bike? Then the three of us throw the washing machine in last.'

'OK, I'm game,' said Dee. 'Alice?'

'Cool. And the rest of dad's stuff that's downstairs?'

'Some of it we bag up for the bin men, then maybe we could get your father to send a cab over and the driver can take it to the council tip, wherever that is?'

'Camden Town.'

Mark's scheme was duly adopted. It went without a hitch and without any intervention from the builders who'd hired the skip. The three returned to the house to survey what remained in the basement.

'Why don't I come by first thing tomorrow – say around nine – and we'll start bagging up? I'll pick up a couple of rolls of heavy-duty bin liners on the way.'

Dee and Alice agreed to the strategy and Mark set off to catch a bus back to his Euston hostel.

X

Caroline Square

ALTHOUGH Mark's taxi dropped him outside the house in Caroline Square at nine sharp, he was surprised to discover that the two women had already been hard at work for more than an hour.

Dee had begun bagging up Kaz's files and paperwork, although Alice seemed more absorbed with reading old copies of *World of Interiors*, which she quickly classified as 'uber-retro'.

Mark set to, filling the new supply of black bags he'd brought with him, and by mid-morning it was possible to see at least fifty per cent of the front room's floor, which turned out to be covered with chocolate-brown vinyl tiles.

'How would it be if we made a stack up against that wall in the area outside, beside the steps up to the pavement?' Mark suggested. 'Then when Kaz sends the taxi we can pass them up to the driver?'

'If it comes,' observed Alice without looking up from her magazine.

A small mountain of nearly fifty black bags was eventually constructed by Mark and Dee. Cross-legged, Alice read on.

Sipping a mid-morning coffee, Dee decided that if ten bags were set aside for the council refuse lorry, with another ten in reserve for the following week's collection, there was only the mountain outside to dispose of. By 11 a.m. the promised KazCab still hadn't appeared. Mark rang Kasmin on his mobile.

'Been manic down here, mate. I'm afraid three o'clock is the earliest I can spare a driver.'

'Three?' said Dee in exasperation. 'That's no use, Mark!'

'Why not?'

'Well, knowing Camden Council officials, the tip will close at four, which means they start winding down at quarter-to and so they'll probably close the bloody gates at half three! Tell him to forget it. We'll take 'em in my Mini.'

Mark and Dee made four sorties to the nether regions of Camden Town, with black bags piled up across the Mini's back seat and stuffed into the car's tiny boot. When they returned to the house just after two, Alice had left a salad lunch for them and had returned to sunbathing half-naked in the garden.

'What have you got planned for the rest of the day?'

'I thought I'd nip down the Caledonian Road to pick up some paint and brushes and a roller and see whether the hardware store can recommend a reliable locksmith.'

'Would you like to stay for supper?'

'If it's no trouble. As a matter of fact, I was thinking of going to the cinema tonight. Would you like to come?'

'What were you planning to see?'

'The Renoir on Brunswick Square is showing Neil Jordan's *Byzantium*. I missed its release when I was in Sicily. Do you fancy it?'

'What's it about?'

'It's a gothic horror story about two un-dead vampires – a mother and daughter – who go around killing men for their blood.'

'Not my cup of tea, I'm afraid, but Alice would love it. She's heavily into vampire horror.'

Ten minutes later Alice wandered in to collect a Coke from the fridge. 'Have you seen *Byzantium*?' her mother asked.

'No, why?'

'Mark's going tonight and wondered if you'd like to go.'

'The one about the mother-and-daughter vampires? Cool. What time do we need to leave?'

'The film starts at eight. It's at the Bloomsbury Renoir, so we could walk it if you like?'

'Cool.'

'I'll have supper ready for six and then you two can set off just after seven. It's a nice walk from here; I've done it. Head for Marchmont Street, opposite St Pancras Station.'

After the early supper Alice announced that she was going to change. Thirty minutes later she called down from her mother's bedroom: 'OK to borrow your skull T-shirt?'

'Sure, but get a move on!' Dee replied, as she and Mark stood waiting for Alice in the hall.

'Come on Alice, or you'll be late for the movie!'

Eventually she appeared, wearing a replica of the famous Alexander McQueen 'skull' T-shirt over a hip-hugging pair of scarlet Capri pants with matching suede ballerina pumps. The space between them was slim bronzed calves, with a thin silver chain around the left ankle. She stopped two steps from the bottom of the staircase to be admired.

'I don't think the ankle chain's a good idea, darling.'

'Why not? My friend Jan wears one. In fact she sometimes wears three!'

'Judging by what I've heard about the 'activities' of your friend Janice, I'd say three ankle chains was highly appropriate! Now take it off.'

'Please?'

'Off!'

Alice dutifully removed the chain and dropped it into her mother's outstretched cupped hand. Dee followed them to the front door. 'And behave yourself at the Renoir.' Turning to Mark she added: 'My daughter has been known to shout "boring" at the screen if the action flags!'

On their walk back to the square after the movie, Alice enthused about the acting of the two female leads and even tried to make a comparison with her mother and herself. 'Hey, Mark – can't you just see it? Mum and me, creeping around Somers Town, preying on unsuspecting pensioners? Drinking blood from their necks? And wasn't that finale just *so* gross? I've never seen so much Kensington gore!'

They arrived at the house just after ten. Alice, who had now officially certified the film as 'awesome', began to regale her mother with details of the goriest parts. 'Then in the final scene they all fetch up in this funfair, right? And the mum and daughter are up against two un-dead baddies, called The Brethren. And…'

'I think I'd stop there if I was you,' Mark interjected, 'otherwise your mother won't get any sleep tonight.'

Alice thanked Mark for the cinema trip and slipped off to bed. Dee poured Mark a second glass of wine. As she walked back to the fridge she called out: 'Would you like to stay?'

Her question hovered in the air. Mark urgently tried to discern whether it was an invitation to use the spare room, or to share Dee's bed.

'Err, that's very kind of you, Dee. But as I'm due to check out of my hostel tomorrow morning, I think I'd better get back.'

'Fine'. He detected a tinge of disappointment in her answer.

'Bad call', Mark thought. 'Selfish, bad call.'

She followed him into the hall to see him off. 'Mark, thanks again for all your efforts today. And for taking Alice to the movies. I really appreciate it.' She moved slightly closer as she expressed her thanks.

'You're very welcome. She's good company, your daughter…'

He froze on the spot as he detected the unmistakeable aroma of orange and cinnamon, merged with church incense, swirling around in the still air.

Dee studied his face closely. 'You OK?'

'Sure. Someone just walked over my grave, I expect. All right if I come by at about ten, after I've checked out and settled up at the hostel? I could make a start on the painting.'

'Of course. That would be fine. See you tomorrow.'

It was nearer eleven when Mark turned up at Caroline Square, having decided that, at the very least, he needed to have something to sleep on. That morning he had visited a Muji store near Tottenham Court Road and bought a cheap futon, which he carried slung over his back in its hessian sack.

After a quick coffee in the kitchen with Dee, he descended to the basement to plan the decorations. As he was laying out the equipment for the tedious preparation jobs, there was a knock on the door connecting with the staircase to the hallway. Alice entered, bare-footed and wearing her One Direction T-shirt and a very short, pleated pink tennis dress. Her pink-dyed hair-do now had added emerald green highlights.

'Hi there, Alice.'

'Thanks for the movie last night.'

'You're welcome. I enjoyed it.'

She slumped herself down in the matching half of the striped sun loungers and began composing a text message on her iPhone.

'Your mum tells me you're due to start college in September.'

'Yeah.'

'Where?'

'Bermondsey Multi-Media.'

'What subjects?'

'Social Networking Data Visualisation.'

'With a view to what?'

'Oh I'll probably go and work for Google down the road, then start up my own company and retire when I'm thirty.' She delivered this encapsulated career strategy in much the same way as a newsreader summarises the next day's weather at the end of a news bulletin.

Alice tapped on and Mark continued with his preparation.

'Who are you texting?'

'My boyfriends.'

'Boyfriends plural?'

'Yeah.'

'How many?'

'Three'

'Why d'you need three boyfriends, Alice?'

''cause I'm trying 'em all out.'

'For what?'

'Sex.'

'I see.' He paused to concentrate on a tricky crack in the plaster-work. 'And how are your road tests going?'

'Rubbish. I reckon the whole thing's over-rated.'

'Really?'

'Yeah. Seems to be over in about ninety seconds flat!'

He squeezed some Polyfilla from its tube. 'Well that sort of thing can often happen with young men. It's called...'

'Yeah, yeah, I know', Alice snapped irritably. 'Premature ejaculation. So I'm thinking of trying someone a bit older.'

'Really?'

'Yeah. Fran my best mate's going out with a bloke who's thirty. Reckons their sex is like really hot.' Then, after a short pause: 'How old are you?'

'Thirty-seven. Bit too old for you, I guess.'

'Oh I don't know.' She glanced up from the phone momentarily, eyeing him up and down. 'But you'd need to smarten yourself up a bit, mate. Is this unkempt appearance deliberate or are you slobby by nature?'

'Bit of both, I suppose.'

She looked disparagingly at his boots. 'And beige trainers, Mark: they're like so fucking yesterday!'

He ignored the slur and carried on with his filler. Alice returned to her texting.

'Wanker!'

He put down his filler knife and tub. 'Now what's up?'

'Jezza says he wants to watch a fucking *Top Gear Special* with his mates tonight! I'd rather watch paint dry!'

Mark resumed his filling. 'Well tomorrow you can.'

'Can what?'

'Watch paint dry. I'll be painting these two rooms'.

'No way!' More aimless tapping. 'Err...Mark?'

'Yes, Alice.'

'How'd you like me to give you a bj?'

'A what?'

'A blow job, stupid!'

'Err, I don't think that would be a terribly good idea.'

'Why not?'

'Well for starters, if your mother found out, I'd be out on the street within the hour.'

'Well she's not likely to find out, is she?'

'Why?'

'Because she's down Sainsbury's doing the weekly shop, and it always takes her at least three hours! Mum goes into a total trance when she gets into a supermarket. It's truly bizarre. I can get round all the aisles in quarter the time.'

Mark was mildly relieved that the subject had moved from fellatio to supermarket shopping techniques. He carried on working silently.

Alice wriggled on her sun lounger. She swung her legs round and planted her bare feet at either side on the floor, opening her legs provocatively. It was obvious even from the other side of the room that the girl was wearing no knickers.

'Did I tell you about my other best friend, Janice?'

'No, I don't think you've mentioned her.'

'Gives the guys at her college blow jobs in the toilets. Charges a packet of ten fags a time. Then sells them on, discounted, to kids who smoke. I think that's so cool.'

Mark didn't respond. What with the constant flow of thinly-disguised innuendo and the occasional views of Alice's snatch, he was starting to get hot under the collar.

'Fancy making me a mug of tea?'

'Sure. In a mo. What d'you think about my business plan?'

'Business plan? Sorry, I think I missed that bit. What business plan was that?'

Alice snapped back in exasperation: 'My plan to start up in bj competition with Jan! Free market economy and all that bollocks. Trouble is, I need to like get in a bit of practice. Is it difficult?'

'Is what difficult?'

But Alice's question remained unanswered, as a terrifying crash resonated from the outside area below the street.

'Christ, what was that?' asked Mark, dropping his knife.

'Kids, probably,' replied a disinterested Alice, tapping the screen of her phone.

'Kids? Doing what?'

'How should I know. Go and see.'

Mark moved over to the basement door, unbolted it and opened it gingerly. The entire paved area – at least six square metres – was covered in white emulsion paint. The door to the old coal cellar was ajar, and an empty paint can stood upturned in the coal dust. A second tin remained undisturbed on a wooden shelf inside the cellar space. Alice, now standing behind him, seemed mystified by the carnage.

'Can you get me a large bucket from upstairs please? I'd better get this shifted before it sets. And a large stiff-bristled broom if you can find one?'

'OK'. Alice padded off upstairs while Mark gingerly skirted the wreckage without treading paint into the room.

Half an hour's concentrated cleaning had most of the emulsion washed away down the outside drain.

Supping their belated mugs of tea, Mark asked: 'So do you really think local kids could have done that?'

'Sure.'

'How come there were no white footprints on the steps?'

Alice just shrugged. 'Search me.' Without looking up from her phone, she added after a short pause: 'It could've been Tibby.'

'What, your cat?'

'Yeah, why not? She's always mouse-ing, especially in that cellar.'

Just then they heard a car pull up in the street above. Shortly after, Alice's mother called down to her from the hall.

'I'd better go and help Mum put the shopping away. Catch up with you later.'

It was only after the girl had slipped off upstairs that Mark recalled that when he had stored the two cans of emulsion in the coal cellar the day before, he had carefully slid the door's bolt home securely.

He worked on for an hour without interruption and was toying with the idea of having a break and walking round to the local chippie, when there was a tap on the door leading upstairs to the hall, and Dee appeared holding her cordless phone.

'Kaz on the line for you, Mark.'

'Hi Kasmin.'

'How's it going, mate? Glad to hear you and Dee fixed up a deal.'

'Not bad, not bad at all. I'm decorating. Still prepping; planning to get on the emulsion roller at the crack of dawn tomorrow.'

'What have you got planned for Monday?'

'Monday? No idea. The Job Centre, I suppose.'

'How'd you like to do a day's driving for KazCabs?'

'Is that allowed?'

'Anything's possible in the minicab game, mate. So long as you've got a clean current driving licence?'

'Sure.'

'It's just that one of my drivers is going off on maternity leave.

She wasn't due for another fortnight, but she's just phoned in to say the hospital's told her it could arrive early next week, so I'm bloody snookered. Fancy your chances on London's roads?'

'Don't see why not.'

'Great. Well, get yourself down here for 7 a.m. sharp next Monday morning and I'll show you the ropes. Got a great first booking for you, a real toff. Good tipper too.'

'You're on. I'll be there.'

'Well done, mate. Have a good weekend.'

'And you.'

Mark padded up the rickety stairs to return Dee's phone. She was stretched out on the sofa, eyes closed, listening to some Chopin. 'What did his lordship want?'

'He's offered me a day's mini-cabbing next Monday.'

'And what did you tell him?'

'I said I'd give it a go.'

'Well, you just make sure he pays you, Mark. My ex can be conveniently absent-minded when it comes to settling debts!'

XI

Sunday at Granny Sutton's

AS HE WAS rolling up his futon just after eight the following morning, Mark heard a loud knock on the front door upstairs.

A few moments later, there was a gentle tap on the door at the inter-connecting staircase. He swung it open to reveal Dee standing barefoot, her loosely-belted cotton dressing gown barely covering her body. She was bra-less and her miniature pink knickers revealed that she didn't believe in women shaving their private parts. 'Your lock-smith's here.' She smiled, seeing Mark staring directly at her crotch, but made no move to cover herself. 'I sent him round to the front area. He's fetching his tools from his van.' She went back upstairs.

Mark let the locksmith in from the outside area. He turned out to be a cheery Cockney, aged around fifty.

'Morning, squire. Sorry to be so early, it's just that we're chocker with orders at the moment.' In one hand he clutched a box marked Yale and in the other a large blue tool box. 'Where's it going?'

'This outside door here.'

'Right you are.'

Mark returned to packing his futon, then breakfasted on fruit juice and a KitKat. Shortly after, he heard the front door slam shut and assumed that Alice had been sent on an early-morning errand.

Around ten, as Mark was settling up with the locksmith, Dee appeared, now dressed in her signature dungarees and T-shirt. 'Fancy a croissant, Mark?'

'Thanks, Dee. That would be smashing.'

He showed the locksmith out via the outside door, whose new security lock made a satisfying clunk as its latch slid home.

Dee was sitting in the kitchen, but there was no sign of Alice.

'Alice having a lie-in?'

'No, she's gone over to visit her friend Janice. Then they're going to Camden Market and she says she'll probably sleep over. What are your plans?'

'I'm going to press on with the prepping and then try to get the first coat on this afternoon. Tomorrow I'm going over to Kentish Town to see my grandmother, to collect some personal belongings I left with her before I went to Sicily. I'll try to get the second coat on when I get back after lunch. What are you up to?'

'Oh, I've got a bit of cooking to do, then I thought I'd take in the Mary Quant exhibition at the V&A; this is its last weekend. Afterwards, I'll drop in on an old uni friend who lives behind Harrods. I probably won't be back 'til late.'

'This is yours by the way.' Mark had been turning over three shiny keys in his hand and slid one across the table. 'It's the new outside door lock from the basement area.'

She slid it back. 'No, it's your flat, so it's your front door.'

He pocketed the keys and nodded his thanks. 'By the way, I haven't forgotten – I'll let you have your first month's rent tomorrow if that's OK?'

'Sure, whenever. Time for another coffee?'

'Just a quick one, then I'm going to finish the prepping. By the way, where's your nearest IKEA?'

'Miles away, out on the North Circular. Would you like me to take you?'

'It's just I've had an idea for an economical way of fitting some basic storage units and a shelf for a microwave alongside that old Belfast sink. I figured IKEA would probably have something in flat-pack form.'

'We've got one of their catalogues kicking around here somewhere.

I'll dig it out for you tomorrow. Maybe we could go over there together one day next week?'

'That would be good. Right, I'm going back downstairs. If I don't see you again, have a lovely day at the V&A.'

He heard the front door slam shut just before noon. It seemed strange being in the big house on his own and in between the noisy bursts of scraping and sanding, Mark was aware of the myriad creaks and groans which an old house makes in repose, with wind draughts, cross winds and minute climatic changes all producing responses from the timber-based structure. At one point, he stopped the sanding of some plaster filler, convinced he'd heard descending footsteps on the connecting staircase, though he was sure Dee had left an hour before.

By lunchtime he had finished. He swept up all the mess, depositing the used sandpaper and newspapers in an extra black bag which he put in the outside area ready for the council's Monday morning refuse collection. Not wishing to trespass into Dee's domain upstairs, he let himself out by the basement door and walked around the corner to buy some cod and chips from the local chippie.

In the afternoon, he put in four solid hours of emulsion painting with a roller, then slid open the barred sash window at the front to speed up the drying process. It had turned very warm, and though he was tempted to abandon the job for the day and go for a good long walk, he decided that painting the skirtings and door frames with gloss was more important. He finally cleaned his brushes at 6 p.m., just as the front door banged shut and Dee called out, 'I'm back.'

He delayed going upstairs for half-an-hour, then when he heard her moving around in the kitchen decided it would be in order to go up. She was sitting at the kitchen table, nursing a large glass of retsina. Barefooted, she was wearing a pretty blue-and-white striped Breton-style top and white jeans.

'Want to come and have a look?'

'In a mo. Have a drink with me first.' It was obvious that Dee had already had several herself. She poured him a glass. 'Anyone call or ring?'

'Nope. It's been very quiet. I've got the first coat of emulsion on and I've glossed all the skirtings and door frames. I haven't decided about the doors. I even had time to go round the corner to get some fish and chips for my lunch!'

'My, you have been busy.' She looked slightly dejected.

'How was the exhibition?'

'Great, but it was terribly crowded. It's my own fault; I should have gone weeks ago. But the visit to my friend Lizzie was a disaster!'

'Why?'

'I'd only been there half an hour when her current lover turned up, unannounced. Sleazy-looking oik, the sort that wears heavy gold chain bracelets? They couldn't get rid of me fast enough so that they could spend the afternoon shagging!' She looked close to tears. 'And I hadn't seen her for yonks.' She topped up their glasses.

After a long pause, she half-smiled and asked: 'So tell me about Sicily? You've been keeping remarkably quiet about your visit, Mr Sutton. Got any pictures?'

'They're still in my camera and I can't download them 'til I collect my laptop from my grandmother's.'

'What's the island like?'

'Absolutely beautiful, Dee. You'd love it. Take Alice. The people are friendly and the food is superb. But don't go after mid-May 'cause it can get terribly hot. I got a nasty dose of sunstroke and was laid up for nearly three days with a fever.'

'Where was that?'

'In the convent.'

'And what was it like – being surrounded by nuns?'

'Oh they're just lovely; so kind and very hospitable.'

'Young or old?'

'Oh, they're all ages. Only nine in the Order, plus the Mother

Superior, of course.'

'Any good-lookers?'

'It's very hard to tell, in their wimples. They all look alike, with their angelic oval faces. There was one that I got on especially well with.'

'Oh my God! Don't tell me – you haven't fallen for a nun?' Mark stared down at his wine.

Dee's suppressed tears welled up. 'You have!'

He looked up plaintively, half-smiled and confided: 'Sort of.' Now they were both filling up.

'And what's her name?'

'Beatrice.'

'Pretty name. How old?'

'Eighteen.'

'Strewth. And where is she now, still at the convent?'

Not so much looking as listening, Mark slowly moved his head, first to the left and then the right. It was as if he was checking that there was no-one else in the room. Then, like the curious moment in the entrance hall three nights before, he detected the faint aroma of orange and cinnamon merged with incense. It hung in the air in the kitchen. It was as if there were three of them sitting at the table.

'To tell you the truth, Dee, I'm not really sure.'

Nursing a mild hangover, Mark awoke in the basement at seven the next morning. He was delighted to note that in the quiet of the Sunday, he could just make out the distant peel of church bells. All was quiet upstairs and he decided that Dee was probably also suffering the after-effects of an excess of wine.

As he didn't have to be at Granny Sutton's until noon, he decided he would tackle the journey northwards to Kentish Town on foot to clear his head, taking in a segment of Regent's Park. At Primrose Hill, he was spoilt for choice with several classy cafés and patisseries serving early breakfasts. Over a latte and a bacon-filled croissant, he wasted a good hour browsing the quality Sunday papers.

Along the length of a subdued Kentish Town High Street, he finally made Attlee House just before noon and rang one of the numbered buttons set in a steel panel by the glass entrance door.

'Is that you, Mark?' a frail voice enquired.

'Yes, Gran, it's me! I'm downstairs.'

'Come on up.'

The door release gave a long buzz and he went in. A much-faded photograph of the post-war British Prime Minister, Clement Attlee, was the all-white hall's only decoration.

Mark rode alone to the sixth floor. The lift doors opened to reveal a stooped and elderly old lady, one arm holding an ivory-handled walking stick, standing in one of the four entrance doors which opened onto the landing. She wore a blue and purple, floral print dress, with a turquoise necklace and matching ear studs. She beamed as she caught sight of him as he stepped from the lift to embrace her. In little more than a month her stoop seemed to have become more exaggerated.

'How wonderful to see you, Mark. Home safe from Italy?'

'Sicily.'

'Sicily, of course, silly me. I'm getting terribly forgetful. Come on in. Lunch won't be long.' She moved forward very slowly across the polished wooden floor, then stepped to the left into a neat and compact kitchenette. An aroma of roasting lamb permeated the little flat. She called out: 'Go on in to the sitting room and pour us both a nice glass of cream sherry, will you dear? It's in a decanter on the sideboard.'

Mark stepped into the brightly-lit space. Propped up against the cut glass decanter was his postcard of Caravaggio's *The Madonna of the Rosary*. He placed a large box of After Eights in front of it.

'Found it?'

'Yes, fine Gran. Don't worry about me. I'm just going to admire the view from your balcony.' He set her glass of sherry down on the connecting serving hatch.

The sound of a saucepan lid hitting the floor, accompanied by an apologetic 'oops', made him smile, but he resolved not to ride to the rescue of this independent eighty-year-old. 'Won't be long,' she called.

He stepped outside. Midday, and the view was spectacular, with the dappled emerald green downs of Hampstead Heath spread out like a patchwork quilt. A soft breeze blew in from the north, making the big picture window's thin net curtains billow out like clouds.

'Can you take these hot dishes for me, dear? I'll pass them through the hatch.' There then followed four, perfectly prepared, matching serving dishes of vegetables and a platter containing neatly-carved slices of roast lamb covered by a thick gravy.

Granny Sutton emerged from the kitchen looking a little flustered but rather satisfied. Slowly and without the aid of her stick she edged towards the armed dining chair set with its back to the balcony window. She gestured to Mark to sit opposite her, then took a small sip from her sherry glass. 'Help yourself, dear. Mint sauce is in that bowl. And what is this?' She looked down at a green tissue-wrapped object set on her bread plate.

'A little gift from Sicily, Gran.'

The old lady gingerly unwrapped a small, hand-painted ceramic bowl with raised geometric patterns in a vivid palette of reds, oranges and ultramarines.

'Oh it's beautiful! Thank so much, Mark.'

They began their Sunday lunch together silently. Mark hadn't eaten a prepared meal like this since returning to England, and although wearied by the effort, his grandmother had clearly enjoyed its preparation.

'This is absolutely delicious, Gran. You've surpassed yourself!'

'Thank you, dear.' She carefully laid her knife and fork on her plate and looked towards him. 'So tell me, Mark: did it do you good – your rest in Sicily?'

He continued eating and then replied in a non-committal way: 'Yes, I think so.'

She pursued her quarry. 'Are you signed off from that Dr Whatshisname?'

'Lundt, Dr Lundt. Technically, no. He said to go to see him when I got back.'

'And will you?'

'I expect so. Next week, perhaps.'

'And what about the medication he prescribed?'

'Well Gran, to tell you the truth, I forgot to take it with me.'

She shook her head and re-commenced eating. 'Well, you be sure to tell him that when you go to see him next week. When you've had all that support from our hard-pressed National Health Service, I'd say the very least you can do is finish the treatment!' She set her knife and fork down, as if to emphasise the reprimand.

'Yes, you're probably right. I'll ring him tomorrow.'

As he looked up towards his grandmother, intending to reassure her of this pledge, his eye was caught by a movement over her shoulder. He'd left the balcony door ajar and the incoming breeze was fluttering the net curtains behind her in hypnotic swirls. Suddenly, across the balcony outside, he saw a white-clothed figure moving sideways, as if trying to conceal itself. Bent forward in motion, it was identical to the profile of a nun moving towards a prayer rail in a chapel. His knife and fork crashed onto his plate.

'Mark! Are you all right, dear? You've gone quite pale!'

He stared straight ahead at the window. 'Can I... just go and check outside? On the balcony?'

'Whatever for, dear?'

'Dunno. I thought I saw someone moving around out there.'

He jumped up and opened the balcony door directly behind his grandmother's seat. He stepped outside onto a deserted space, looked around and then re-entered the living room.

'I could have sworn there was someone out there.' He brushed his hand across his grandmother's shoulder in reassurance. 'Trick of the light, I suppose. Sorry.'

But as Mark re-took his place at the dining table, he noticed that the warm smell of roast lamb and mint sauce which had pervaded the living room for the last hour was now overlaid by the familiar aroma of orange, cinnamon and incense.

Calm was partially restored by his grandmother's other speciality: rhubarb and apple crumble with ice cream. Though the incident on the balcony was not alluded to again, he sensed the old lady's anxiety over his strange behaviour.

'So you've found yourself somewhere to stay, have you?'

'Yes, Gran. Friend of a friend's rented me a couple of basement rooms.'

'Where, dear?'

'Somers Town. Behind King's Cross Station.'

The old lady wasn't impressed. 'Somers Town? Dear me, in my day, you didn't dare walk through there, even in the daytime. And at night, you'd as like as not get your throat slit!'

'It's a bit different now. Creeping gentrification has arrived.'

'What does that mean? I don't understand all these modern slogans.'

'It's a sort of half-way house between slum living and posh respectability.'

'I think I prefer Kentish Town. At least you know where you are here.'

'Has the family always lived up here?'

'Your great-grandfather – my father – once lived near where you're talking about, down at King's Cross. He was a collier – worked out of St Pancras for the Midland Railway. They had a workman's cottage just off the Caledonian Road. I was born there.'

'And what did great-grandmother do – apart from bring up the family?'

'Katherine – Kitty she was always called – was very emancipated, actually, and a committed suffragette.'

'I never knew that.'

'Oh yes. Quite militant was my mother.' The old lady chuckled to herself. 'There was even a family rumour that Kitty became a member of the Suffragette Movement's unofficial arsonist wing, which used to go around setting fire to public buildings.'

'Really?'

'The Orchid House at Kew was their biggest coup. It was in all the papers. Of course Mrs Pankhurst had to officially disown them, but dad knew she'd done it. I'll see if I can dig out some old newspaper cuttings for the next time you visit.'

'That would be good, Gran.' He put down his pudding spoon. 'Thank you so much for looking after all my goods and chattels for the last month. I'm sorry if they've been an inconvenience, cluttering up your spare room.'

'Not at all, dear. It was no trouble; I was happy to oblige. How are you going to get them back?'

'I'll ring for a cab.'

With Mark's help, the old lady cautiously manoeuvred the empty dishes to the kitchen's serving hatch but insisted on attending to the washing-up alone.

From the flat's spare room, he began transferring his belongings into the hall by the front door. There was his laptop computer, a box of art books, rolled-up posters, a miniature music centre and CDs, two carrier bags full of winter clothes and his beloved Caucasian runner. When he put in a call to KazCabs he got a recorded message asking him to ring back.

He wandered into the kitchen and presented her with the chocolates. 'How nice, my favourites. We'll have one with our coffees.'

'No luck with the mini-cab service I rang – probably because it's Sunday afternoon. In a while I'll go downstairs and see if I can get a black cab.'

They sat quietly together on the sofa drinking their coffees.

'And you'll be sure to ring your doctor tomorrow?'

'I promise.'

Hoping the medical interrogation was over, Mark moved to get up to go and look for a taxi, but he was out-foxed.

'Mark, if there was anything that was still troubling you, you would tell me wouldn't you?'

'Of course, Gran.'

'It's just that you really worried me at lunchtime, rushing out there onto the balcony like that.'

He put his cup and saucer down on a table beside the sofa.

'Well, since I've been back – what is it, a week now – I have had one or two strange experiences.'

'Strange? In what way, strange, dear?'

'Inexplicable things. Things that seem to have no logical explanation.'

'I don't follow.'

'That's the trouble, neither do I. I hear footsteps, yet there's no-one there. Sometimes floorboards creak when the house is empty. Then the other night a huge tin of paint mysteriously fell off a shelf, spilling white emulsion paint everywhere. And then there's this strange perfume which follows me about.'

'What sort of perfume?'

'It was here today, in this room – didn't you smell it?'

'No, dear.'

'Just after I dashed out on the balcony? Cinnamon and orange. Heavy and musky, like church incense. And always... always it comes just when I've been thinking about...' He tried to choke back the tears, but failed miserably. Limply he keeled sideways, sobbing on his grandmother's shoulder. They sat together quietly, then resting his head on the sofa cushion, Mark nodded off.

He resurfaced after a while and saw that his grandmother had placed a cup of tea by his side. She shuffled in from the kitchen.

'Do you really need to go back to your flat tonight, Mark? Wouldn't you be better off staying here? I can soon make up the spare bed.'

'That's kind of you to offer, Gran, but unfortunately I'm committed to doing some mini-cab driving for a friend tomorrow, and he wants me to start at seven.'

'That's awfully early isn't it? Does anybody really need a mini-cab at seven o'clock in the morning?'

'He's got to show me the ropes, so to speak. Says he's got some good bookings – special clients who tip well. And as it was him who gave me the introduction to the person I'm renting the flat off, I can't really let him down, can I?'

'No, I suppose you can't.'

Mark finished his tea and rode down in the lift with the first batch of his possessions, stacking them out of sight in an alcove in the entrance hall. After three trips he had brought everything down to street level except his treasured runner. He stood on the sixth floor landing clutching it vertically at his side like a guardsman's rifle as he said farewell to Granny Sutton.

He rode down in the lift to the entrance lobby, collected his belongings and set about finding a black cab to take him back to Caroline Square.

XII
Soane Museum

WITH SUPERHUMAN effort, sustained only by a chocolate bar, Mark made it to KazCab's offices by 7.05 a.m. the following morning.

Parked on a double yellow line outside the adjoining betting shop was a chrome yellow Porsche Boxster coupé, bearing the distinctive registration number DI NAZ.

Kasmin was in the front office sat at Dina's desk, checking through some drivers' dockets. 'Chop, chop, old son, five minutes late for your first day's work? That'll never do.'

'Sorry Kaz. Late night and all that.'

'Oh yes? Where were you? Not out with that gorgeous cross-dresser from the Granby, you old dog?'

At that early hour it took Mark a moment to recall his encounter with the mojito-swilling Linda the week before. 'No way! I was up at my gran's in Kentish Town, collecting some stuff I'd left with her while I was in Sicily.'

'Right, let's get started. Your first pick-up is at 8.50 in Regent's Park, so let's go round the corner to the compound and take you through the controls on one of the Skodas.'

Five minutes later, after unlocking two fearsome-looking security padlocks and swinging back a pair of rusting corrugated iron gates, they beheld the entire KazCab fleet: twelve orange Skoda hatchbacks, neatly parked in two echelon lines. They took the front seats in the first one and Kaz dropped the driver's manual onto Mark's lap.

'Five-speed manual with power steering. Diesel. Dead easy to drive, but check in there if there's anything you don't understand.' He clicked a shallow grey metal box onto clips in front of the gear lever. 'That's your float. Fifty quid in small change, right? Keep all the doors locked at all times, whether you're in the cab or helping a little old lady into Selfridges. London's full of light-fingered toe-rags these days.'

He pointed to a pump by the gate. 'Fill up before you go out and that'll keep you going all day, so you won't need to re-fuel. Unless, of course, some punter decides he wants you to take him to Cardiff!'

'How does the fare system work?'

'It's all on the driver's display – mileage rate, miles covered and the cost of the journey. And it's duplicated on Dina's console in the office, so no hanky-panky, Mark!'

'As if I would.'

'No, mate, I know you wouldn't. And when you bring the float back tonight – the release key's on your key fob – we split it 60:40 – 60 for me 'cause I'm paying for your fuel, 40 for you. Your two-way intercom with Dina is top right and there's also a hands-free cradle on the dashboard for your mobile. All driving offences and parking tickets are strictly down to the driver. And if you have a knock, never admit liability. Never!'

'And tips?'

'Keep whatever the fare gives you. These days, some of them are mean bastards – especially with the return trips from the supermarket, where they've just put £75 on the plastic. Some – like this guy you're collecting from Regent's Park this morning – can be very generous. Lebanese ladies are said to be *numero uno* with my drivers at the moment. That's about it. Let's go and grab a quick coffee back in the office, then I've got to get Dina's car back.'

Kasmin sat on Dina's desk reading from her diary, while Mark parked himself on a plastic stacking chair in the corner, with a note pad and pen.

'Right, mate: now don't mess this one up! Sir Giles Lomax QC.

Done me some good favours – and KazCabs. Lives at 34 Cumberland Terrace, Regent's Park. Going to 9 Lincoln's Inn Fields. Pick-up 08.50. He's dead arsey about pick-up times, it's always to the minute. I reckon he's allowed the best part of an hour to get him to some top-drawer lawyers' meeting, probably with a 10 a.m. kick-off. Going south, the left turn into Lincoln's Inn Fields is off Southampton Row just after Holborn Station. It's a one-way and looks no wider than an alleyway. Miss it and you'll be half-way over Waterloo Bridge before you can do a U-turn. Got it?'

Baffled, befuddled with instructions and still only half-awake, Mark replied: 'Got it.'

Kasmin chucked him the key fob. 'Right, I'd better go. See you around six. Good luck!'

Mark checked his watch: it was just after eight o'clock. He decided he would head over to Regent's Park and take a couple of turns around the park to familiarise himself with the Skoda's controls, but after fuelling up the mini-cab he realised he had barely half an hour to get from King's Cross to Regent's Park and locate the famous lawyer's home.

He pulled up outside No. 34 at 8.52 a.m. to find his first fare standing on the front steps of an impressive four-storey town house, peevishly consulting a pocket watch.

Mark jumped out and opened the rear door for him. 'Good morning, Sir Giles. Lincoln's Inn, isn't it?' His passenger climbed in uttering a grunt, which Mark took to be confirmation of their destination.

Fortunately the traffic was light and flowing freely and the little Skoda was running like a well-oiled sewing machine. The famous lawyer made three mobile calls, all to someone called Ursula, who Mark decided must either be the wife back at Cumberland Terrace, or the receptionist at Lincoln's Inn Fields, or his mistress. The fourth – an incoming call – confirmed the final suspicion.

'Darling, I've told you: Diana wants us to accept the Chequers invite, just so she can rub shoulders with a bunch of eastern European *parvenus*! We're going to have to make it the following weekend I'm afraid, my sweet.'

Mark was so engrossed in his eavesdropping that he almost missed the turning and had to brake sharply, causing Sir Giles Lomax's mobile to fall on the floor. 'Sorry, sir – it was the idiot in front.'

They finally pulled up in front of the Lincoln's Inn address at 9.57 a.m. Three minutes in hand on his first job. Mark jumped out as a flustered Sir Giles was retrieving his phone from beneath the driver's seat.

'I'm going to be about an hour and a half in there,' he barked haughtily. 'Then I have to get over to London City Airport for a 14.00 hours flight to Brussels. D'you mind waiting, or shall I get a black cab when I come out?'

'No, of course I don't mind waiting, Sir Giles.' Mark gestured to the kerb enclosing Lincoln's Inn Field's central park. 'I'll park over there, by the gates. See you at 11.30.'

'Right you are.' He strode off to do his costly legal business.

Mark breathed a sigh of relief and climbed back into the driver's seat. He was dying for a cappuccino – or even an energising double-macchiato – but the park's coffee cabin was still boarded shut. He toyed with the idea of walking back to Southampton Row. Ninety minutes to kill. Leaving the mini-cab unattended on his first outing worried him, and there was certainly no point in ringing in to Dina for another fare. He sat in the stationary car studying the well-dressed female passers-by, listening to mind-numbing Classic FM.

A blue-uniformed porter, carrying a small wooden notice board, came down onto the pavement from a terraced house opposite. After he had retreated into the house, Mark got out, locked the car and strolled over to read its message. 'Soane Museum. Opening hours: 10.00 a.m.-5.00 p.m. Entrance free. Please form a queue as admission numbers are restricted.'

The door to the museum was open and since there was no queue, Mark climbed the steps and went in. As he entered the narrow entrance hall, the porter was setting out a visitors' book on a side table, together with souvenir guides and postcards. 'Good morning, sir. Would you mind signing our book?' he asked courteously. Mark placed a £5 note on the desk and picked up one of the guide books.

He moved slowly down the hall. He was the first visitor and had the pick of all the rooms, in what appeared to be a spacious Victorian gentleman's residence, complete with authentic furniture and paintings.

The large salon overlooking the square seemed the logical starting point for his tour, but as he walked into the room he noticed a cleaning lady was uncoiling the flex of a vacuum cleaner. He moved diagonally across the room towards a sign reading 'To The Monk's Parlour'. A panelled passageway, hardly wider than the width of his shoulders, connected to a narrow spiral staircase with a worn iron handrail, which led down to a dimly-lit basement.

The first area he arrived at, signed 'The Crypt', was dominated by a huge Egyptian sarcophagus resting on an iron-wheeled trolley. Looking down on the space was a bronze head of Pluto and the walls were hung with macabre curios such as death masks and leg irons. The emptiness of this dank and gloomy space with its associations of death made him decide to move on.

Suddenly he detected the familiar scent of cinnamon and orange, lingering in the damp atmosphere... the now-familiar signal that his lover was close at hand. Through a round-headed stone arch, he perceived a smaller, alcove-like space, lit by a shaft of morning sunlight coming down from a high-level skylight. The light falling on the tiled floor was dappled with blood-red blobs from the roof window's stained glass.

The Monk's Parlour certainly looked more inviting than the Crypt. It was about five metres square, with book-lined shelves and architectural miniatures dotted between the ancient leather-bound volumes. To one side, partly in shadow, was a small, octagonal rosewood dining table and four crimson velvet-upholstered chairs. And on the far side, in the alcove's deepest shadows, a beaming Beatrice was seated. Shafts of grey light seemed to envelope her white wimple.

Without rising, she opened brightly: 'I knew you had an hour to kill before your wealthy lawyer returned, so I thought a discreet museum like this would be just the place for our first meeting in London.'

Mark stood before her, dumfounded. He leaned forward, taking her outstretched hands. 'I've missed you most terribly.'

'And I've missed you too, dearest Mark. But I've been watching over you, just as I promised.'

'Really?'

'You don't suppose straw hats grow on trees? Remember my promise to you in the convent bedroom?'

He thought back to all the other unexplained moments during the last ten days when he'd sensed her presence.

'Or tins of paint jump off shelves?

'That was slightly different: an emergency.'

Standing before her, Mark placed his hands on his hips petulantly. 'Beatrice, it was utterly childish!'

She shrugged coquettishly. 'Desperate times call for desperate measures. Isn't that the saying?'

'The other night with Alice? What was so desperate?'

'I should keep your voice down, dearest. No-one else can hear or see me, so the porter upstairs is quite likely to think he's let a nutter in!'

Sotto voce, Mark repeated: 'What was so desperate about the other night?'

'That little minx was flirting outrageously with you!'

'Harmless teenage fun.'

'Then why did you look up her skirt?'

'Human nature, I suppose.'

'You did know she wasn't wearing any knickers?'

'I had noticed.'

'What you *didn't* know was that shortly before she came down to see you, she went into the bathroom to take them off. *And* I was there when you were flirting with her mother!'

'You mean when her mother was flirting with me.'

'Same thing. Did you know she'd even changed the sheets on her bed that afternoon?'

'Could we change the subject please?' Mark took a deep breath, drew out a dining chair and sat next to Beatrice at the table.

She smiled affectionately at him. 'Of course. But Mark, dearest, be warned: we redheads are fiercely possessive!'

At that moment two American tourists entered the Monk's Parlour. The man held a video camera aloft, like an advancing US trooper in Fallujah; the woman clasped the museum's official guide in front of her like a hymnal. She looked up when she saw Mark, seated alone at the table, mistaking him for a curator.

'Excuse me, sir, but is this the Crypt?'

'No, next door.'

'Why thank you so much.' They shuffled off.

'Beatrice – can you explain something to me?'

'I'll try. What is it?'

'Well, though you seem to be all around me and with me a lot of the time – I often sense you are close – why is it that I've seen so little of you since we made love together in the convent?'

'It's not always possible – for a variety of reasons that would take all morning to explain – for you to actually *see* me, even though I may be present. In simple terms, there are 'degrees of visibility', if you follow?'

'And why are your visits so tantalisingly rare and brief?'

She took his hand in hers, stroking it softly. 'I've *told* you, darling: it's out of my control.'

'Don't they ever let you stay out overnight? Why can't we spend tonight together in my flat?'

'Not allowed. It's in our regulations. They don't like us bonding too closely.'

'So what about our night together in the convent? If that wasn't bonding, I don't know what is!'

'Computer glitch. That's why I had to disappear before it got light. I'm sorry, sweetest.'

'Supposing...' Mark couldn't properly frame the words to disguise his intentions. He slid his hand away from hers. 'Supposing... supposing something was to happen to me?'

She gently stroked the nape of his neck. 'By "happen", I assume you mean die?'

'Suppose I got run over by a bus or something, would that make it easier for me to see you?'

'In the after-life?'

'Yes. In this nether region you inhabit, which seems to be bound up by more rules and regulations than the EU!'

'Mark, you have to remember the after-life is infinite. It's not Brighton! The chances of us ever meeting up are just about nil. In fact, I'd say the odds of you bumping into Esbjörn Svensson are probably greater.'

The Americans shuffled past the parlour's entrance on their way upstairs, the woman giving Mark a suspicious look.

'May I ask you a personal question?'

He looked dreamily into her hazel brown eyes. 'Ask away.'

She rested her head lovingly on his shoulder. 'Would you ever sleep with another woman?'

'Of course not!'

'Not even Dee, if she comes down to your flat tonight in that flimsy cotton dressing gown of hers, with nothing on underneath?'

'No, I wouldn't, I promise.'

'How about a quick blow job from little Alice?'

'Don't be absurd! Beatrice, you're my only love.' He kissed her affectionately, first on the cheek and then, as she turned her head towards him, slowly and passionately on her lips.

When they had composed themselves, he asked: 'And have you ever slept with anyone else apart from me?'

'Only once.'

'And who was that?'

'A pastor who was visiting our convent from the Vatican.'

'And?'

'He seemed very... troubled. I think he was gay but was too ashamed to own up to it, so I visited his room. And we made love.'

'In my bedroom?'

'No, of course not.'

'Where?'

'In the big bedroom down the corridor from yours.'

'The one with the pink baroque ceiling?'

'Yes, the one you were sketching.'

'So it *was* you I heard outside on the landing?'

'Yes.'

'And you never saw him again?'

'No. He was terribly contrite about the whole thing and when he got back to Rome he made a full confession to one of the cardinals. Three weeks later they sent him off to Equatorial Guinea as a missionary.'

'Seems rather a harsh punishment for a one night stand.'

'That's Vatican double standards for you.'

'How did you discover all this?'

'I saw his letter to Reverend Mother lying open on her desk one day – but he hadn't told her about me.'

Mark leaned back in his chair and pointed the face of his watch to the light. It showed 11.26 a.m. 'Christ, I must go. Lomax will be champing at the bit!'

'I must go too.'

'So when will I see you again, Beatrice – I mean properly see you, like this?'

'Who knows? I'll try to make it very soon, my love, I promise. And I will always watch over you.'

They left the museum together, with Mark bounding down the outside steps two at a time. Following him, the hem of Beatrice's swirling habit clipped the queuing post, causing it to mysteriously crash on the pavement in front of the small clutch of visitors who were waiting to go in.

Mark dashed across the road to find an irate Sir Giles, his bulging briefcase under one arm and a hand clamped impatiently on a locked door handle. Across the roof he passed Mark a parking ticket. It said he had exceeded his stay in the square by four minutes.

'Oh Christ, I'm so sorry about that!' Then clicking the central locking to admit his passenger: 'Right, London City Airport, wasn't it?'

Mark made good time across London until they were in sight of the new city airport complex, then they were fed into a slow-moving convoy which passed a seemingly endless line of traffic cones protecting roadworks, although no-one was working. As a result, the Skoda pulled up outside the airport's departures hall with a very irritated Sir Giles Lomax having just twenty-five minutes to check in and catch his Brussels flight. He slammed the rear door, rasping, 'I'm an account customer', and sloped off without giving Mark a tip.

Mark manoeuvred the Skoda into a short-stay car park and was about to ring in to Dina when the back door was yanked open by a swarthy-looking Eastern European with a laptop bag slung over his shoulder.

'You free, mate?'

'Err... sure, jump in,' stammered Mark, deciding he needed to make up for some of the morning's lost revenue, although he could really have done with a fifteen-minute, post-Lomax recuperation.

'Take us to the Mile End Road, will you? Anywhere near the tube station will do.'

'Right you are, squire.'

This seemed an altogether better prospect than the curmudgeonly

Sir Giles. Mark even toyed with the idea of swinging into a bit of cabman's argot but in the end decided to play his passenger Classic FM's all-time hits.

When they were still a good mile away from the tube station, they caught a red light on a pedestrian crossing. As Mark was poised to move forward, the back door opened and his fare ran off without paying. Three fares and the float still untouched.

After parking in a side street in Bow, Mark decided to honour the undertaking he'd given his grandmother and put in a call on his mobile to Dr Lundt. He was kept waiting for more than five minutes listening to Vivaldi's 'The Four Seasons', before a receptionist announced: 'I'm afraid Dr Lundt is unable to speak to you at the moment, Mr Sutton. He says if you will give him a time when he can reach you, he'll try to call you later today.'

'What time does he leave the surgery?'

After a pause and more snatches of Vivaldi, the voice returned: 'It looks as if his last appointment is at 6 p.m., so I guess he could ring you at around 6.30 p.m., before he goes home, if that would be convenient?'

'Yes, that's fine, tell him. He's got my mobile number.'

'Very good, Mr Sutton, I'll make sure he gets the message.'

After locking the Skoda and checking that he wasn't infringing local parking regulations, Mark took a late lunch in a greasy spoon. He kept a low profile, staying buried behind his copy of *The Spectator* on realising that most of the café's other customers were black cab drivers. After his brief lunch, he walked into the Mile End Road and located a branch of his building society, where he withdrew £400 to pay his first month's rent.

He strolled back to the Skoda forty minutes later, feeling considerably better than he had in the morning. A light flashing on his dashboard indicated that Dina wanted him.

'Where've you been, Mark?'

'I had to take Sir Giles out to London City Airport after his meeting. Then I stopped for a bite to eat.' He decided it would be prudent not to mention the Mile End runner.

'You're supposed to call in when your fare books you for a second journey.'

'Sorry.'

'Right, can you take this down? Mrs Bloom. Three o'clock sharp pick-up from 88 Queens Grove, St John's Wood, to go to Selfridges. She's a regular. Likes to be dropped at the store's side entrance in Orchard Street, so she can go and have a salt beef sarni in their brasserie. Got it?'

'Wilco, Dina.'

Mark set off for north London, deciding to use any spare time until he picked up Mrs Bloom parked up on Regent's Park's inner circle, chilling out to Classic FM and forgetting about how cantankerous Sir Giles had ruined his tryst with Beatrice.

Shortly before 3.00 p.m., the Skoda's sat nav located Queens Grove, which ran between Avenue Road and Finchley Road, at the Swiss Cottage end of St John's Wood. It was known as the 'gefilte fish quarter' by some taxi drivers.

Mrs Bloom was waiting for him, smartly attired, standing on the front porch of an impressive Edwardian villa. She was wearing a fluffy white angora sweater and a full-length black silk skirt over black leather high heels. Around her throat was a stunning three-string pearl choker. Mark hopped out and opened the rear door.

'Good afternoon, madam. Selfridges, I believe?'

'That's right.' She climbed in, trailing a voluminous leather handbag and smelling of expensive perfume.

'My dispatcher tells me you like to be dropped off at the Orchard Street entrance?'

'Yes please, dearie.'

Mark had a salivating Mrs Bloom ready to get stuck into her salt beef sandwich in less than thirty minutes.

'Pick me up from the front entrance in three-quarters of an hour, will you dearie? I need to get some perfume.'

Mark slowly cruised around Mayfair and dutifully notified Dina of his return booking. 'Might as well come in after you've dropped Mrs B off, Mark. It's gone all quiet.'

'Wilco'.

Two hours later, he was locking the Skoda away. After returning the float to the office, Mark set off to walk home, fingering Mrs Bloom's £10 tip in his pocket: his sole reward for a harrowing introduction to mini-cabbing.

He bought himself a KFC chicken-nugget-and-chips bucket en route. As he came out of the takeaway it started to rain and he held his magazine over the bucket to keep his supper dry. He briefly stood in a bus shelter to consume some of the nuggets. On the shelter's back wall was an illuminated Samaritans poster which read: 'Whatever life's done to you today, we're here to listen.'

His lightweight anorak was now letting in the heavy rain and he decided to eat his cold, soggy chips in the open in Caroline Square. He sat on a wet bench facing No. 25. The lights on all three floors were on, with no curtains or blinds drawn. Alice was mooching around aimlessly at the top of the house, dressed only in a skimpy T-shirt; Dee, in her dungarees, was ironing on the floor below; and the sitting room was deserted except for Tibby, who sat on the window sill surveying the square.

As he was letting himself in from the basement area, an incoming call on his mobile showed that Dr Lundt was on the line.

'Mr Sutton? Thomas Lundt. I believe you rang the surgery earlier. How can I help?' Mark closed the outer door and stood in the centre of the basement's front room, dripping wet but trying to remain calm.

'I haven't been in touch for a while because I've been abroad. I think I need to come and see you again.'

'Are you having problems?'

'Sort of.'

'Do you want to tell me about them now?'

'I'd prefer to describe them to you face-to-face.'

'I understand. Let me just get my bookings schedule up on the screen. I'd turned my computer off, so it will take a couple of minutes. Tell me, are you still taking the tablets?'

'No, that's part of the problem.'

'Did they produce an adverse reaction?'

'No. It's just I forgot to take them with me to Sicily.'

There was a long silence. Mark wasn't sure whether this was an indication of the psychiatrist's annoyance at his patient's absent-mindedness or whether he was merely scrolling through his appointments. 'I see. That's unfortunate, Mr Sutton. It was a specially-formulated, high-dosage course, which included steroids. If you remember, I did emphasise that it was very important for you to complete the course.'

'I know. I'm very sorry, Dr Lundt.'

'Interrupting a medication treatment like that can easily produce side-effects.'

'What sort of side-effects?'

'It's difficult to generalise. And it would be unwise of me to speculate before seeing you again.'

'I understand.'

'When can you come in?'

'Tomorrow?'

'Unfortunately tomorrow is fully booked. And the following day I'm speaking at a medical conference in Bristol. Thursday afternoon's the best I can do.'

'OK, I'll come over on Thursday. What time?'

'Say three o'clock. I'll need to arrange for some tests and it may even be necessary to send you for a scan, so expect to be here most of the afternoon.'

'Scan? What for?'

'As I've said, Mr Sutton, your medication contained powerful drugs. Discontinuing them prematurely may – I emphasise may – have had an adverse effect.'

'Right. OK, I'll come to the surgery at three on Thursday.'

'Very well. I'll bid you goodnight, Mr Sutton.'

'Good night, Dr Lundt.'

XIII

A Call for Help

SHORTLY BEFORE midnight, Mark was awoken by the distant sound of a police car's siren. The house was quiet and there was no noise coming from the square. He reached over to finish the last drops from a giant bottle of mineral water, then climbed out of the futon to fill the bottle with tap water from the sink in the corner.

As he moved back to regain his rumpled bedding he was struck by the amazing geometry of a long angled shaft of moonlight entering from the back skylight. It diagonally dissected the room, falling across the Caravaggio poster he'd blu-tacked that morning to the panelling beside the door leading to the interconnecting staircase.

The poster was a faithful reproduction of the famous *St Francis of Assisi in Ecstasy*, showing a prone Francis (claimed by art scholars to be a self-portrait of the artist) being comforted by a winged angel. The two figures appear in a darkened arbour, with the merest hint of moonlight falling on the surface of a pool in the background. In his art school thesis Mark had drawn attention to the picture's vivid example of the dark-light contrast technique – known as *chiaroscuro* – which Caravaggio had pioneered.

There had been moments in the past – even in his student days – when this poignant picture, with the intense intimacy of the two interlocked figures, had almost brought Mark to tears. Tonight it gave him thoughts only of death. In her caring tenderness, the angel was Beatrice and the figure of the entranced saint, his head in the angel's lap, was Mark. After death.

He climbed back onto the futon but couldn't get back to sleep, re-visiting his conversation with Dr Lundt and puzzling over what 'certain tests' might involve. Almost certainly more medication. Perhaps electronic brain scans?

The slogan on the bus stop poster kept going round in his head: 'Whatever life's done to you today, we're here to listen.' He tracked the Samaritans' national helpline through his mobile and keyed in the number. After three rings the call was answered by a softly-spoken female voice – possibly Asian, he guessed.

'Samaritans. Can I help you?'

He was lost for words.

'You're through to Samaritans.'

Still silence at his end.

'Take your time, if you're finding it hard to talk at the moment.'

Mark rehearsed an opening statement in his head, but he just couldn't deliver it.

'My name is Usha. Please tell me how I can help you tonight?'

He wanted to tell her – he desperately wanted to tell this kindly-sounding woman – that his name was Mark and that he'd reached the end of his tether, but not a word of it emerged.

'I am happy to wait until you're ready to talk. Can you hear me all right?'

Mark pressed the red 'end call' button and slid the phone under his pillow. It was now nearly 2 a.m., but sleep wouldn't come. He got up to fetch the water bottle from the draining board and to use the loo.

He scooped the phone from under the pillow and pressed its re-dial command. Three rings again and then a male voice announced: 'Samaritans. Can I help you?' This time the voice sounded more businesslike; a clipped accent from somewhere up north.

'You're through to Samaritans.'

'Hello?'

'Hi, my name's Phil. How can I help?'

'Err... I'm not sure. I don't really know where to begin.'

'Try to tell me what's troubling you.'

'How long have you got?'

'As long as you like. That's what we're here for.'

'My name is Mark, by the way.'

'Hi Mark.' He was starting to sound a little bit more friendly now.

'Where are you exactly, Phil?'

'Where? Manchester.'

'However did I fetch up in Manchester? I'm in London.'

'I shouldn't worry about it; it's the automated call delivery system we use. You ring our national number and the system routes your call to the nearest available Samaritans branch.'

'I see.'

'So try to tell me a bit about what's troubling you, Mark.'

'I don't think I can go on.'

'Do you mean go on with this conversation?'

'No. I mean go on living.'

There was a noticeable pause as Phil digested this statement.

'Mark, I have to tell you that's a remarkably frank thing you've been able to say. I admire you for your candour.'

'Thanks. That's how I'm feeling right now.'

'And can you tell me, Mark, whether it's just an abstract idea – this lack of purpose – or have you given any thought to actually ending your life?'

'The latter.'

'I see.'

'Do you not feel, perhaps, that in the cold light of day – as they say – things might not look so bleak?'

'Possibly. I must say, I've hardly had any sleep.'

'Could that be a contributing factor, do you think?'

'Possibly.'

'Have you spoken to anyone else about your concerns? Your partner, for example?'

'I haven't got one.'

'A doctor?'

How does this guy know how to press all the right buttons, Mark wondered. 'I'm due to see one on Thursday. If I make it to Thursday, that is.'

'Well it's virtually Tuesday now, so you could say there's only two days to cope with. Have you made an appointment?'

'Yup.'

'What is he – your GP?'

'No, he's a shrink.'

Once again, there was a pause as Phil assimilated this information. 'Sounds like you're doing the right thing, Mark: tackling your problem in a logical way.'

'But I don't think I'll be there, Phil.'

'Be where – at the shrink's?'

'Yes.'

'Why not?'

'Because... because I'll be gone.' He pressed the 'end call' button again and collapsed onto his pillow, quietly sobbing.

XIV

King's Cross

IT WAS DAWN. Mark let himself out of the basement flat by the door and climbed the steps to the wet pavement. The overnight rain had stopped but the grey clouds above presaged an incoming downpour. He posted Dee's rent envelope through the front door letterbox. On its reverse he had written: 'Sorry this is a day late. M x'.

Hardly anybody was about. He cut across to Granary Square, avoiding the drifting spray from the water feature. Then down the long pedestrian hill towards the back of the new King's Cross station complex. Small clutches of students and office workers were already coming up the hill. Most carried the obligatory cardboard coffee mug and most were either sending texts or listening to music on their mobile phones. The giant building sites remained unlit and empty. As he neared the station, the heavens opened. Mark pulled up the hood of his waterproof jacket.

Under the cover of the station's space-age concourse, with its lattice-framed roof, he bought a cappuccino from a Costa trolley. The camp barista's 'Have a nice day' was insincere in itself, but the prolonged eye contact was rather unsettling. He sauntered aimlessly onto the front precinct, where a line of early God-botherers were already distributing booklets, trying to engage people in conversation. There were no takers.

He moved into the old main line terminus and sat on an ice-cold steel bench, facing the arrivals and departures screens. Not that he had any intention of travelling to Grantham or Peterborough or York.

He had made up his mind: his destination was the after-life, where he intended to join Beatrice.

In a semi-detached house in Walthamstow, Denise Brookes was up and about, preparing for another seven-hour shift as a driver on London Underground's Victoria Line. When she had showered and dressed, she took mugs of tea to her two children's bedrooms. Fourteen-year-old Jade was still fast asleep; but twelve-year-old Jason was sitting on the edge of his bed in his school uniform, putting on his socks and shoes. She set the mug down on his desk. 'Ta Mum.'

On her final trip upstairs, Denise took her sleeping husband Ted his tea, then she collected a thin waterproof over-garment from their wardrobe and went back downstairs to prepare for her ten-minute scooter journey to London Transport's Northumberland Park depot.

Calling softly up the stairs, 'Goodbye, kids!', she let herself out quietly and moved around to the car port at the side of the house, where her moped was parked. She took her helmet from the pillion box and strapped it on. Four attempts to start the Peugeot all failed. She checked her watch and realised that even if she was lucky enough to catch a bus straight away from around the corner, she would never make it to the depot by eight. But a fifth press on the starter button, accompanied by a mumbled curse about the French, had the machine bursting into life. She wheeled it across the pavement and out onto the road, noting the greasy surface. It would probably take more like a quarter of an hour to get to the depot, she decided, as she eased her ample frame onto the seat.

At King's Cross, as Mark flipped a rubbish bin closed, a fervent God-botherer swooped down on him: middle-aged, wearing a crocheted, pill-box hat in Rasta colours. Her bulk was emphasised by a voluminous patchwork, milkmaid skirt. 'Old enough to have protested at Faslane, probably even Greenham Common,' Mark supposed. She held out a small booklet entitled *Jesus Wants To Save You*. Mark took it and turned it over with half-hearted curiosity.

'You know Jesus wants to save you, friend?'

He handed the booklet back to the woman. 'I think I'm past saving.'

'None of us is past saving, friend. None of us!' Extending her arms sideways with a theatrical flourish, she added: 'We are *all* God's children!' One or two station-bound commuters hastily veered away; they weren't going to get involved at this hour. Addressing them as they fled, she cried: 'COME TO THE LORD!' Mark fled too.

Against a tidal wave of exiting office workers, Mark moved across into the underground station's crowded booking hall. There were long queues at all the five windows of the ticket office, so he fished in his pocket for some loose change to purchase the cheapest ticket to get him through the automatic barriers and down onto one of the platforms. He crossed to a newsagent and bought a Kit Kat. Once through the barrier he joined the escalator which was descending to the Victoria Line's north- and south-bound platforms.

Because the crowds seemed thinner and a little less frenetic, he branched right at the bottom of the escalator and followed the signs for Brixton. The long, curving platform had just been emptied of passengers and the overhead indicator panel showed that the next train was due in two minutes. To avoid being swamped by alighting commuters, Mark took a seat at the far end of the platform. It was as close as he could get (without alerting suspicion) to the entrance to the tunnel from which the trains emerged. But he had already been picked up on a CCTV monitor in the station's central control room.

In east London, Denise was nervously concluding her moped ride to the train depot. The roads were treacherously greasy and outside the Odeon she locked up the back wheel and did a side slide, just managing to keep the Peugeot upright. The driver of a black cab going the opposite way stuck his hand out of the window and gave her a thumbs-up. She took this as a compliment: from her experience on London's roads, taxi drivers' contempt for scooter riders was only exceeded by that for cyclists.

By the time she had parked and locked the moped, storing her helmet and waterproofs in the pillion locker, it was 7.55 a.m. In forty minutes she was due to collect her eight-carriage set for the first run to Brixton.

The staff canteen was close at hand and she calculated she just had time for a coffee and a couple of sausage sandwiches. It was hot and crowded. She paid for her meal and took her breakfast tray to a table at which a distinguished-looking Indian inspector, wearing a RMT union lapel badge, was sitting. 'Mind if I join you, Raj?'

'Please do, Denise. Nice to see you.'

Denise sat down and hungrily attacked the first of the two sausage sandwiches.

'And how's old Ted, these days?'

'Bit grumpier, I suppose,' she replied with her mouth half-full. 'Still misses the buses.'

'Nasty business, wasn't it Den? Our union rep was such a useless bastard at that tribunal. He should've got your Ted off with an official written reprimand, not the bloody sack!'

'I know, I know.' She finished the first sandwich.

'You managing moneywise? What with you being the only wage earner now?'

'Just about, but with two hungry kids to feed, it ain't easy, I tell you Raj!'

'How old are they now?'

'Jason's twelve and Jade's fourteen.'

'Nice looking girl, your Jade.'

'Too nice!' She tucked into the second sandwich.

'How d'you mean?'

'She's up the duff!'

'Christ! Does Ted know?'

'Nope, not yet. And to cap it all, she wants to have the kid, would you believe?'

'Fucking hell, Den! Excuse my French.'

'Don't worry mate, I've said worse than that!'

Denise bolted the remains of the second sandwich, swilling it down with coffee. 'Hey, I'd better shoot off, we're out at 8.35 a.m. Keep what I just told you under your hat, won't you, Raj?'

'Of course I will Denise. You take care now.'

She dashed to the locker room next door to collect her travel box and security keys, then went down the staircase onto the platforms, where a row of gleaming red and blue Victoria Line trains were standing in parallel lines. She slipped on her treasured khaki forage cap, a souvenir of a Cuban Solidarity Brigade work camp.

Denise walked briskly along the platform to the first carriage, down its central gangway and unlocked the internal door to the driver's cab. It was 8.31 a.m. It only took her two minutes to settle into the cushioned driver's seat and go through the security checks. The three front windows were spotlessly clean and as the entire journey was underground there would be no problems with the light rain which was still falling. She engaged the automatic traction control and the train hummed into life. Her route out of Northumberland Park – a non-passenger station – was down to Seven Sisters on a loop line, then back to Walthamstow Central, where the service officially commenced. At Walthamstow she would 'change ends', moving down to the duplicate driver's cab at the front of carriage eight.

Eight minutes later, Denise brought the train slowly into a crowded, south-bound platform at Walthamstow Central. After locking the cab's internal door, she moved along the platform to carriage eight. As she settled into the new seat, she checked in her driver's box that she had brought her heartburn tablets, as she was already feeling discomfort in her stomach. She transferred the box of tablets to her jacket pocket. Maybe confiding in Rajan hadn't been such a good idea, she mused.

After closing the doors, she pulled the combined traction control lever forward out of the arm rest, simultaneously bending its hooked end through ninety degrees, and eased the train out of Walthamstow Central at exactly 8.35 a.m.

In the King's Cross central control room, a message was being relayed to the deputy station superintendent that one of the station's brand new escalators was playing up.

'What exactly seems to be the trouble?' Jack Graham asked down his two-way radio link.

'Number nine's overheating.'

'Just remind me: which is nine? I still haven't got used to the new configuration.'

'Nine's Viccy down.'

'Is there a duplicate alongside?'

'No boss, that's eight, Viccy up.'

'Shit! Well get onto Kone. Tell 'em we want engineers down here soonest.'

'Right you are, boss.'

One of the CCTV observers stood silently at Jack Graham's elbow, holding a scrap of paper. 'What is it, Nigel? It'd better be important because we're just about to have an escalator malfunction.'

The thin, insignificant young man stared down at the note. 'It may be nothing, boss, but there's a geezer sat on a bench on Victoria southbound, and he's let four trains go through without attempting to board.'

Graham decided that, with all his other problems, this wasn't yet a life-threatening event. He wanted to get on with harassing the engineers who had installed one of his new escalators, before it came to a grinding and costly halt.

'Perhaps he's waiting for his girlfriend – or boyfriend. Maybe he doesn't like crowded carriages. Keep an eye on him and if he hasn't moved on after three more trains, send – oh, I don't know – send Jasmine down to talk to him. She could charm the birds off the trees.'

He swung his desk chair through 180 degrees, jumped up and strode over to the door marked 'Station Superintendent' to alert his chief that an emergency was probably in the offing.

The train which Denise carefully drew out of Walthamstow Central was carrying around 300 passengers. This number was likely to increase by anything up to 200 per cent by the time she reached Oxford Circus, regarded by all the drivers as the halfway mark on their thirteen-mile route.

Outside Finsbury Park, she got held up by a red signal and took the opportunity to get out her box of Gaviscon tablets. Just as she'd discarded its outer plastic wrapping, the green light indicated for her to proceed into the deep, north London tube station. She rode in slowly. Not too many waiting passengers, she noted. And not many would be alighting at this hour. She'd likely as not make up half a minute with a quick in-and-out. So she thought. But she hadn't reckoned with the irregular operation of the wheels of an ancient luggage trolley being pulled by a tiny Chinese lady attempting to board her train.

The woman first managed to get the wheels of her mobile wardrobe stuck in the gap between the carriage and the platform edge. Then the energetic actions of a couple of Australian tourists in the carriage caused the entire contraption to burst open, depositing Chinese female attire onto the platform, the carriage floor and down the gap between.

From the CCTV monitor on her central console, Denise had the facility to view both ends of all of the eight carriages. An Asian platform attendant, running forward to assist, flashed up three fingers to the driver. She hit the button three times to bring up an image of the chaos in the carriage, not helped by the fact that the distraught Chinese lady's underwear was now being viewed by half of north London.

Denise switched on the cab-to-carriage live announcement channel and reached for her heartburn tablets. 'Sorry for this slight delay, ladies and gents. We should be moving forward to Highbury & Islington, King's Cross and Euston very shortly'. Then, like a teacher admonishing her class for ignoring a school rule, she added: 'Items trapped in doors can cause delays.'

She slipped the foil card containing the oval tablets from the carton and placed it on the console beneath the big central window. Then she pressed the button which connected her with the control room at King's Cross.

'Sorry guys. We're still at Finsbury Park. A Chinese tourist has just deposited her entire wardrobe on the fucking platform. At least five more minutes please? Sorry.'

Back from a frosty interview with his boss, Jack Graham reassured Denise. 'No probs, driver. We're experiencing minor technical difficulties here as well. One of the escalators may be out of service by the time you get to King's Cross. We'll keep you notified.'

'Thanks, control.'

The Finsbury Park station staff had the Chinese lady's entire clothes collection in a dirt-covered pile in front of her as she sat weeping on a platform bench. Then the Asian platform attendant waved a white signalling paddle, Denise closed the doors, and her train slipped away.

From experience, she knew that the next section of tunnel was one of the longest on the entire route. She decided to make another attempt to get at her elusive heartburn capsules. The cab bucked slightly on a rail connection, causing the precious card to be dislodged from the console and it fell on the floor. 'Shit, shit, shit!'

At King's Cross, Mark sat forlornly wondering why the Victoria Line's southbound service seemed to be delayed. His platform was filling up rapidly and the indicator board showed a flashing 'Delays' sign. At that moment, one of the vortex-like downdraughts of warm air, which mysteriously occur on the underground system, suddenly blasted onto the platform from an exit arch close to where he was sitting. It carried with it the unmistakable perfume of cinnamon, orange and incense.

Jolly, overweight Jasmine had no problem weaving her ample body through the throng, always smiling and murmuring: ''scuse please? Thank you. 'scuse please?' As she approached the far end of the platform, she spotted the 'loner' she'd been told to check, but he was no longer alone. She saw he was deep in conversation with a nun. They appeared to be bent forward, in earnest dialogue. Jasmine clicked on her walkie-talkie.

'There's a nun talking to him, boss. Seems to be holding his hand. Shall I leave it?'

'Yeah, I'm sure she'll look after him. Looks as if we're going to have to shut down escalator nine, so stand by to get passengers off the southbound platform and re-direct them down the Piccadilly tunnel.'

As the crow flies, Highbury to King's Cross is less than three miles. That's the distance cattle drovers would have had to cover on their way to the capital's huge Smithfield meat market. It would have taken them a good half day. A quarter of a mile beneath this route, in a smooth, purpose-constructed tubular tunnel, a Victoria Line train will comfortably reach speeds of 50 m.p.h. and cover the distance in twelve minutes. Denise had now given up all hope of any heartburn relief before Brixton. The foil capsule card rattled tantalisingly on the cab floor.

Suddenly, her control-to-cab system cut in. 'Driver: we've had to shut down the up escalator at King's Cross. Please advise any disabled passengers, or passengers with heavy luggage, that they should proceed on one stop to Euston. Understood?'

Denise was less than a quarter of a mile away from King's Cross and still going full throttle. She eased back the traction control lever. 'Wilco'.

She switched on the live cab-to-carriage announcement circuit. 'I've just been advised that there is no up escalator in operation at King's Cross, which is our next stop. Disabled passengers and passengers with heavy luggage are advised to travel on for one more stop to Euston. Once again, apologies for the inconvenience this morning, ladies and gents.'

In the confusion of all the incoming messages and announcements, Denise had inadvertently left her cab-to-carriage channel open.

Through the dimly-lit section of tunnel running down from Highbury & Islington, the bright lights and white tiles of the King's Cross platform suddenly hove into view. In concentrating on making her escalator announcement, she had let the train proceed too fast over the final section. It appeared like a thunderbolt from the tunnel mouth, the steel-on-steel banshee wail announcing its arrival.

On their bench by the tunnel's entrance, Mark and Beatrice huddled together, their faces touching, their bodies intertwined.

There was a sudden dramatic forward movement. A white blur. Denise instantly let go of the red hooked end of her 'dead man's lever'. Then came the diabolical, thundering, bone-crunching impact.

The train's eventual stop was a powerful double-jolt: the kinetic force of several hundred bodies lurching forwards involuntarily, and the agonising fatal contact between the leading carriage's chassis and the two entwined figures who had thrown themselves from the platform.

And broadcast at full volume into every carriage on the crowded tube train was the single, pitiful cry: 'NOOOOOO!'

Down on the southbound platform, the emergency claxon had been silenced. With polished efficiency, the platform staff had shepherded passengers down the platform away from the accident. The train was stranded, with just three and a half of its carriages clear of the tunnel entrance. Within minutes, tall screens had been erected on the platform edge. The bodies, immediately in front of the driver's cab, where Denise remained seated, stunned with disbelief and crying softly, were now covered by crisp, white sheets. The pungent smell of the braking wheels' scorched steel hung in the air.

Accompanied by a railway police inspector and a WPC, three paramedics approached the abandoned underground train from the platform's furthest end. Two pushed a wheeled stretcher.

The lead paramedic gently knocked on the side window of the driver's cab, indicating for her to release the lock. Denise remained looking fixedly ahead, blankly staring at the giant shroud on the track. He shone his torch into the cab and lit up her ashen face. After a second gentle tap he caught her attention and she turned her head towards him, almost in slow-motion.

'Can you make it outside, love?'

It took fully half a minute for her to understand the question. She nodded and slowly rose from her seat. She shuffled unsteadily towards the door to release its safety catch. The heartburn tablets lying on the cab floor popped as she crushed them with her Doc Martens. The paramedic gently pushed the inward-opening access door half open and took her hand. One step down, but she just couldn't make it. Her knees buckled and she fell sobbing into his arms. His two colleagues swiftly moved forward with the stretcher.

After carefully covering the woman driver with three red blankets, the lead paramedic leaned forward close to her face. 'What's your name, love?'

'Denise.'

'Right, Denise. We're going to stay here for a few minutes, then we'll move you down the platform – soon as it's clear of the last of the passengers. OK?' She closed her eyes and nodded.

Up in the station's control room, Jack Graham was trying to juggle with two major emergencies with reasonable calmness. All the CCTV monitors showed the hectic activity which the fatal accident and the escalator malfunction had caused throughout the underground station.

He shouted across to an overweight Indian boy with a shaved head, who was engrossed in a graphic horror novel. 'Denzil – get onto Network Rail HQ. Tell 'em we've got a "one under" and we'll need authority to set up an emotional counselling unit outside on the station forecourt for tomorrow morning. And put that fucking comic away!' After reflecting for a moment he tapped his computer to bring up a contact name. 'On second thoughts, get yourself up to Eversholt House right away. Ask to see this guy – they're to get him out of a meeting if necessary.' He scribbled the contact's name on a piece of paper and handed it to Denzil. 'Tell him we'll need a unit on the forecourt by 8 a.m. tomorrow. He'll do the rest, but you're in charge, Denzil!' The youth scampered off.

Graham glanced across at the furthest in the long line of monitors, showing a wide-angle view of the forecourt of King's Cross Station. A red fire service emergency rescue operation unit had pulled up and parked behind the paramedics' ambulance. Three helmeted firefighters – two wearing bright yellow hats and one in white – in full personal protection equipment were climbing out. After loading tools, ropes, saws, lights and tripods from the back of the truck onto a red trolley, they walked calmly through the watching crowd towards the station, to carry out the recovery operation.

The firemen were escorted to a goods lift, which took them down to the Victoria Line's level, and were then guided through a labyrinth of pedestrian tunnels until they reached the platform where the empty train was standing. They drew their trolley towards the front and began unloading the equipment beside the opened door of the driver's cab.

By now, Denise had been taken to a cavernous store room at platform level. It was eerily silent, save for the hum of the air conditioning and the occasional screech and crackle of the lead paramedic's two-way radio. The WPC was already writing in her notebook. Jasmine, the station attendant, made up the group of six.

The driver's eyes remained closed as one of the paramedics carried out several tests to gauge her level of shock and trauma, then nodded to the inspector, who knelt on the floor to get as close as possible to her.

'Denise?'

'Would it be all right if we just asked you one or two questions? Are you up to it?'

There was a pause and then she nodded, without opening her eyes.

'We've got your personal details from Broadway and your husband Ted has been informed. We've told him you're safe and being well cared for. He's coming here by police car.'

Denise smiled. She rather liked the thought of a sacked bus driver from Walthamstow being driven into central London in the back of a police car. 'And the kids? They'll be back from school soon.'

'Not just yet, love. It's still only 9.30 a.m. But I'll get a WPC to call at the school in the lunch break. Ted can give us the details when he arrives.' The inspector looked up to the WPC, who nodded.

There was a tap on the door and the head firefighter half-entered the room. He gestured with his head for the inspector to withdraw into the passageway.

'I'll be back in a jiff, Denise,' he said.

Outside the store room they moved down the narrow passage to be out of earshot, shook hands and introduced themselves.

'How's it going?'

'Nasty. Very nasty. The junior buck has been sick already. It's his first. Still, no bad thing for him to have a really gory one for starters.'

'How many have you had?'

'First this week. Mind you, it's only Tuesday. I reckon this one's going to take us a couple of hours. Can you let Jack Graham upstairs know that there's no chance of them moving the unit until twelve at the earliest?'

'Sure. I'll get my WPC to radio up to him. Listen, I seem to be getting conflicting reports about the victim. When the call first came through, we were told it was a "one under". Control room upstairs says they first spotted one person – a male – sitting alone on a bench by the tunnel entrance. But the woman platform assistant in there is saying she saw two of them sat on the bench. What's your opinion?'

'No idea. Right at the moment it's just a mess of body parts. We haven't even started bagging up.'

Upstairs, Jack Graham was getting equally confused about the number of accident victims. At his desk, he was quizzing Nigel, the insignificant CCTV observer who'd first drawn attention to the man sitting alone on the bench.

'So have you run the disc back to 08.00 hours?'

'Yes, boss.'

'That was just before you spotted the man sitting on his own on the bench?'

'Yes, boss.'

'Alone?'

'Alone.'

'And?'

'From 08.00 hours to 09.00 hours the disc is blank.'

'Blank? What do you mean 'blank'?'

'It self-erased.'

'So, one CCTV camera out of … how many, Nigel?'

'Two hundred and forty.'

'One camera out of 240 retrospectively wipes all images in the crucial hour leading up to the accident?'

'Yeah, that's about the size of it.'

'Back-ups?'

'We don't keep back-ups, boss. There ain't the storage space. In fact I don't know how we're even gonna store our single copies.' Nigel began to get animated. 'There was a memo the other day – I don't know if you saw it - saying that from now on, we mustn't wipe anything for five years! Came from Scotland Yard's Anti-Terror Unit?'

'Yeah, I saw it.' Jack Graham remained mystified about the malfunctioning CCTV camera.

Working alongside the firefighters, a blue-overalled London

Transport engineer was down in the pit below the rails, examining the state of the lead carriage's bogey and chassis. He climbed back onto the platform, sat down on a bench and wiped his blood-splattered hands on an oily rag. He switched on his mobile phone, eventually making contact with the chief engineer at the Northumberland Park depot.

'Traction control unit's OK – it's one of the 2012 re-cons. Bogey and chassis ditto. We won't need a tow: I'll drive it back to the depot. All the cab's front panels are buggered but the window glass is intact.'

In the store room, a sudden crackle from the paramedic's two-way radio caused Denise to open her eyes. She noticed the tall, uniformed inspector had disappeared and turned her head to face the small, dumpy WPC, who smiled down at her.

'Can I get you some water, Denise?' Denise nodded.

The WPC squatted down beside Denise with a plastic beaker. 'My name's Pat.'

'Call me Den, everybody does.' She swallowed the water. 'When'll my Ted be here?'

'Your husband? Oh, very shortly now, unless they've got held up in the traffic. Whereabouts do you live, Den?'

'Walthamstow.'

'My dad was born in Walthamstow.' Denise gave a half-hearted smile of recognition.

'If you're ready, do you want to tell me a bit about what happened?'

The woman driver then began slowly and hesitantly to recount the sequence of events along the route, following the incident with the Chinese lady's suitcase.

'I know my approach was too fast. The lights came at me real quick – King's Cross can seem ever so bright after you've been in the dark since Arsenal.'

Pat checked her notebook. 'Arsenal? Which one's that, Den?'

'Sorry, Highbury & Islington. A lot of us older drivers still refer to it as Arsenal – that's what it used to be called. Less of a mouthful.

Anyway, I'm looking to see what sort of numbers are on the platform as it was coming up to the peak of the rush hour and we'd already lost time.' She paused to recollect. 'I always keep an eye out for the foreigners – don't know why, but it's mostly large Indian gents – with them giant mobile suitcases. Some of 'em the size of small wardrobes. Then, all of a sudden... Can I have some more water?' She lifted herself up a little on the stretcher.

'All of a sudden there was this like... sideways movement. That's the only way I can describe it. It was like a giant snowball.'

The WPC stopped writing mid-sentence. 'Did you say "snowball"?'

'Yeah. Like a huge snowball it was. You know? Those big ones we used to make as kids? Rolling 'em down a slope until they was as big as us? A bundle of white cloth. And it rolled itself, real quick, to the platform edge. I let go my dead man's lever. Then it hit my fucking train. That's all I remember. Oh, and I think I shouted.'

'This bundle of white cloth? Do you suppose it was wrapped around the bodies of some passengers waiting to board your train?'

'Must've been. How else could it have shot across the platform?'

Pat paused in her note-taking and looked up over her shoulder to see that the inspector had re-appeared and was standing directly behind her. Not knowing how much of Denise's recollections he'd heard, she passed him her notebook. He scanned it quickly, noting that the words 'giant snowball' had been underscored. He moved forward.

'I'm afraid I'm going to have to take you through the last bit of the accident again, Denise. I know these people want to get you to hospital, but can you be certain... this bundle of white cloth you saw? Would it have been covering one person... or two, d'you suppose?'

'Two.'

'Are you quite sure, Denise?'

'Definitely two.' She closed her eyes and shook her head with remorse, then began crying again.

The inspector nodded to the lead paramedic and the team began making preparations to take the woman to the waiting ambulance above. Once they were safely on their way, he went back to the platform. The senior firefighter was taking a break, drinking from a water bottle, his white helmet set beside him on the bench.

'So what have you got for me?'

'Not a lot.'

'One body or two?'

'One.'

'Certain?'

'Certain.'

'How can you tell?'

'We counted the feet. There were only two.'

'Why do you count feet?'

'Because most "one unders" take a dive – so it's their feet which leave the platform last and often escape the impact.'

'Sex?'

'Male.'

'What else can you tell me: age?'

'No idea.'

'Height?'

'Ditto.'

'Colour of hair?'

'Inspector, there's not much of him left!'

'Nothing else at all you can give me?'

'His trainers had orange laces.'

'So we've no idea what this bloke looked like, or how old he was, but he was wearing trainers with orange laces?'

'That's about it, I'm afraid.'

'Fucking brilliant! The media will love it!'

XV

† *Epilogue* †

THE CLOCK on the high Italianate tower above King's Cross Station showed nine o'clock. It was a dazzlingly bright, sunny morning and already warm.

In the centre of the station's pedestrianised forecourt, Denzil was busy laying out literature on a folding table in front of the special Network Rail van which had arrived earlier. There was a high police presence, including several armed officers.

The vehicle, the literature and the staff were in response to the underground accident which had occurred on the station's Victoria Line the day before. The accident was being luridly summarised by the Evening Standard's billboards as: 'KING'S CROSS DISASTER: BODY MYSTERY.'

Jack Graham walked across from his office in the station's control centre. 'Nice one, Denzil, you've done a good job. Samaritans coming?'

'Their Soho branch is sending two volunteers. Should be here any minute.'

'Right, I'm going back to my desk – more accident form-filling, I'm afraid. Give me a shout if you need me.'

'Will do, boss.'

A crocodile of forty, immaculately-dressed schoolchildren in blue and yellow uniforms made its way diagonally across the square. It was lead by a portly schoolmistress, who held her furled blue umbrella aloft as a guidance beacon. Most of the children held hands as they followed her. Two teaching assistants in orange, high-visibility tabards flanked the line and a third brought up the rear.

'School – halt!' called the teacher as she drew alongside the van. 'I wonder if you could kindly direct us to the British Library? We're going to see the Chaucer exhibition.'

Denzil put down his box of leaflets. 'You're almost there. About another 300 yards. Stay on this pavement, go past St Pancras Station and it's the next big building on the right. You can't miss it: all red brick, with green windows.'

'Thank you, young man. School – forward!'

Denzil's first visitor turned out to be a frail and elderly pensioner, who cautiously moved towards the van using a wheeled walking frame.

'Terrible business yesterday, wasn't it? I'm old enough to remember the King's Cross disaster of 1987. Before your time, I expect?'

'Yeah. Read about it, though. A lot of heroes that day weren't there, dad?'

'Lot of dead, too. Thirty-odd I seem to recall. And a brave fire officer. I think he got a posthumous medal.'

As the pensioner was reminiscing with Denzil, a dark-haired, middle-aged man approached on their blind side. He was casually dressed and scruffy enough to be a local vagrant. He glanced at the details chalked on the yellow-and-black incident board which Denzil had set beside the van, then paused in front of the literature display, before taking a Samaritans bookmark. He crossed the square to the shaded wall of the terminus and sat on the end of a long bench. A soiled bundle of rags at the opposite end moved slightly and the man realised it was a dosser, sleeping under an old duvet. Confirmation was the three empty Special Brew cans lying underneath.

The stranger flicked the bookmark aimlessly against his knuckles. A young woman approached the bench unsteadily and slumped down in the space between the two men. She looked directly ahead, then after some minutes took a battered tobacco tin from the pocket of her tunic and began rolling a very thin cigarette.

'Gotta loight?'

'Sorry, I don't smoke.'

She arose rather uneasily and stumbled off to scrounge a light from a commuter. She returned to the bench, slumped down again and took a deep drag on her roll-up. Her dark, lank hair hung over a creased black T-shirt and her pallid face seemed to be washed of all emotion. The man with the bookmark couldn't decide if she was drunk or drugged. She certainly looked as if she'd been sleeping rough.

'Gotta get down the Social. Any ideas where it is round 'ere?'

''fraid not.'

After another long silence she enquired: 'Spare a pound for a cup of tea?'

'Sorry, I'm skint.'

His negativity was annoying her. She stamped out her dog end. 'Don't bother, mate – oi'll go and scrounge in front of the Ladies toilets.'

'Where're you from?'

'What's it to you?'

'No reason. I just thought I detected a Norfolk burr in your accent.'

'Wisbech.'

'Come in by train?'

'No, I flew. Can't you see me wings?'

She decided to postpone her begging and slumped back on the bench with a sigh. She closed her eyes as a woman police officer strolled by, talking into the two-way radio attached to her tunic.

Once out of earshot, the girl opened her eyes and looked cautiously towards the WPC. 'I'm not very keen on being stopped and searched right now.'

Another long silence.

'No work in Wisbech?'

'Not unless you want to stack shelves in Tesco's at night or work in a sugar beet factory. Which oi certainly fucking don't!'

The man saw that the WPC had turned on her heel and was heading back their way. The girl leaned forward, her elbows on her knees, as if about to retch.

The woman constable stopped by the man and nodded at the wasted girl. 'She with you?'

'Yes, officer.'

'She all right?'

'Just a bit tired. Long train journey.'

The policewoman nodded and moved on.

Without rising from her crouched position, the girl mumbled: 'Ta.'

He resumed flicking the bookmark against his knuckles. The irritating sound caused the girl to turn her head towards him. He offered it to her as she sat up. She eyed it suspiciously. 'What's this?'

'Came from that van over there.'

She took it and turned it over a couple of times. To avoid eye contact, she dropped her head and glanced down at his feet. His beige trainers had orange laces.

'Wish I'd let them help me,' he said. 'What's your name?'

'Chrissie.'

'I'm Mark.'